THE AVENGER
AND
THE VOICE

THE AVENGER AND THE VOICE

B F Jochnowitz

STORY
PUBLICATIONS

www.storypublications.com

This is a work of fiction. Names, places, persons, and incidents either are the products of the
author's imagination or are used fictitiously, and
any resemblance to actual persons, living or dead,
businesses, companies, events, or locales is entire-
ly coincidental.

ISBNs [Assigned]
979-8-9868422-4-0 (Paperback)
979-8-9868422-6-4 (Hardback)
979-8-9868422-5-7 (eBook—Kindle)

DEDICATION

TO MY NIECE, SUSAN T.

CHAPTER 1

The Avenger wakens at the usual early hour. After a light breakfast, the closed-tight shutters are opened and the apartment goes through a daily thorough cleaning. Everything must be in its place and squeaky clean. Furniture is sparse with no evidence of clutter or personal items. After showering and dressing, errands are taken care of on the way to work.

Always after dark and dressed in a hooded jacket, The Avenger likes to take a long walk in the area, looking in windows of the neighborhood houses and preferring not to talk to anyone. Anything unusual is checked out—such as trash can covers askew, a light out in the lobby, people arguing in the late night or a dog that should not be barking.

This evening is an exception. The walk is shortened and a plan is being formulated while heading home.

***

Now wearing gloves, thick glasses, black wig, baseball cap and dark tanning lotion, The Avenger whistles a tune while finalizing the task at hand.

***

Henry Dobson called his wife from the office. "Sorry, Hon, but I just found out that I have to go to Atlanta tonight to wrap up a deal with a client."

"Do you have to? Jerry still doesn't feel too great. I hoped that since it's Friday, you'd be home early."

"I did too. But duty calls. I hope to be back by tomorrow night. See you then and tell Jerry I'm sorry."

"Okay. Have a safe trip."

It was so easy to come up with an excuse. One of the best architects at his construction firm, he often consulted with out-of-town clients. His office buddy, Mac, overheard Henry's conversation. "Going to Atlanta huh?"

Henry winked, "What she doesn't know won't hurt her."

Mac looked puzzled. "How do you get away with it? You're always doing this. Are you sure she doesn't know what's going on?"

"Nah, she's so wrapped up in the kid she won't even miss me." Henry stood, took his briefcase and was out the door.

He left his office at the usual time—excited about meeting Pamela at the Colby Hotel's cocktail lounge.

Jerry wasn't feeling too well after breaking his arm, but Henry was sure that Martha could keep him occupied by playing his favorite game of Monopoly. It's the kid's own fault he got hurt. The boy didn't do what he was told. I was just going to give him a light tap. If he stood still and not tried to avoid me, I wouldn't have slammed him against the wall.

Walking toward the parking garage, Henry wondered if Pam would be wearing the earrings he bought her. They were expensive, but she was worth it. Since she started as the new salesperson in his department, he dated her several times. Usually, a quick dinner and a prolonged goodbye at her door. There was never time enough to make love to her properly. But tonight, he planned a very different and romantic evening at the Colby Hotel, and they'd be together most of tomorrow.

With a spring in his step, he hummed a little tune. His car was in sight, so he took out his keys. He reached for the door and a sudden searing pain shot through his back. He saw only black while falling to the cement floor.

CHAPTER 2

Jess gathered her things and started running out of the office. "Crap. I'm late. Can you close up here, Brenda?"

"What's the rush?"

"Got a hair appointment and I should be there by now."

"Sounds like you've got a heavy date. Who is he?"

"No time now. See you Monday."

She screeched out of the parking lot. I hope Sherry waits for me. My hair's a mess. I need a complete style change for tonight. No more frizz.

Driving a little too fast, Jess thought about Sam. We should be at our next level by now. I really like him. He isn't perfect but pretty close. He's funny, gorgeous smile, dreamy eyes, nice physique and a great kisser.

She slammed on the brakes. Damn it. A red light.

Not real tall, but who cares. He's just fun. Nothing more. But why do I have jitters in my stomach?

A loud horn blast broke her out of her daydream. "C'mon lady, get goin'."

"Yah, yah, yah." She waved and moved on.

Jess Gladstone and Sam Wesley met at a wedding a couple of months ago—she, the events coordinator, and he, a guest. He insisted that she dance with him at the end of the evening. Even though she never mingled with guests while working, she couldn't refuse. She thought he was hot, so when he asked her out, she didn't hesitate and said yes. They've seen each other quite a bit since. He insisted on making dinner at his apartment tonight. Maybe tonight's the night.

**

When Jessica opened the door, Sam whistled. "What a knockout!"

She pirouetted to show off her sexy little black dress and spike heels. "You like?"

"I like. Did you get taller?"

"Nope. These shoes are brand new. Couldn't resist them. You're pretty handsome yourself, Sam."

He bowed from the waist and kissed her hand. Jess smiled, "Want something to drink?"

"I don't think so, Jess. Let's get going. Dinner's in the oven."

On the way to the car and under the canopy between two kumquat trees, Jess could feel Sam's eyes on her, so she took longer strides. Her foot slipped on a fallen kumquat and her ankle turned. She fell flat on her face and lay spread-eagled on the pavement.

Sam helped her up, "Are you all right?"

"No, just embarrassed." She brushed herself off and pulled back her shoulders—holding up one of her shoes minus a heel. "And my poor shoe!"

Sam examined it. "Let's go. When we get to my place, I think I'll be able to fix it."

She put the shoe back on, pulled back her shoulders and did a sway-limp to the car. They strapped themselves in, paused for a moment, glanced at each other and burst into laughter. He said between gasps, "You should have seen yourself."

Jess took a breath. "Okay don't push it, Sam."

"How many condos are there in the building?"

"Around 60, I think. That's what I figure from the designated parking spots."

Sam smiled, "Paaking? I do like your New England accent?"

At Sam's apartment, they were greeted by a jumping, excited dog. "Oh, isn't he cute! I didn't now you had a dog, Sam. What's his name?"

"Kugel, and he's sweet and comforting just like my mother's favorite dish."

She started patting and playing with Kugel. "Something smells wonderful."

"It's our dinner. Come to the kitchen. I need to check the oven."

In the kitchen, Jess wide-eyed said, "Sam, what a great room! All this professional equipment. A real chef, huh?"

"Yup. Everything's ready. Go sit down and I'll bring out the food."

When they got to the main course, Sam presented it with a flourish. "Another of my mother's famous recipes."

Jess put the first forkful in her mouth, "Mmmmmm it's good! Did your mother teach you to cook?"

"No, I used to sit at the kitchen table and watch her. One day I tuned to the food channel, and it brought me back. And since I needed a hobby . . ."

"Why'd you need a hobby?"

"Because, at work that afternoon, I saw a guy who died of multiple stab wounds."

"Yuck."

"Right, not a pleasant sight. That's when I knew I needed to do something to relax me. Now I cook. Next time it'll be an Italian meal you'll never forget."

Throughout dinner, they kidded around and relived Jess's clumsy fall. Halfway through dessert, Sam's cell sounded the Star Spangled Banner. That meant a work call. He went to the bedroom and answered.

Frank, his partner, said, "Hi, Sam, can you come down to the station? We've got a situation here, and I need to get your input. The boss wants us to head the investigation."

"Ah, shit! Frank, I have company, and we're in the middle of dinner. She's the real deal."

"Sorry, but I need you, Sam."

"If I die a lonely and decrepit man, it'll be your fault, Frank."

"Jeeze enough with the drama already."

"Okay, okay! I'll be there as soon as I can."

Back at the table, Jessica asked, "What's up?"

"I have to go to work, Jess. I'm sorry and so disappointed."

"It's okay. What happened?"

"I don't know, but my partner said it's urgent. If it isn't, he's a dead man."

He brought out a pair of his slippers. "Put these on and when I get back, I'll work on your shoe." Sam watched her shuffle to the car trying to maneuver his oversized slippers.

At Jess's building, Sam came around to open her car door and walked with a slight limp.

"Why are you limping, Sam?"

"My hip is killin' me tonight."

"How come?"

"Hip replacement. After a gunshot wound. No big deal."

"How awful. Does it flare up a lot?"

"Not often. When it's damp out, I feel a twinge."

Walking arm in arm down the hall, Sam said, "With my limp and your shuffle, we make a very attractive couple. Don't you think?"

"I think you should shut up, Sam." Jess tried to hold back but couldn't. She laughed so hard she started to snort.

He pulled her into his arms and gave her a long, deep kiss.

Jess melted. "Mmmmm, you're good!"

"And I get better."

After he released her, she said, "Thanks for the delicious meal. I had a great time."

"I did too, and I promise to make this up to you. How about next Saturday night?"

"It's a date."

Sam tripped walking down the hall. "I'm okay." He called back to Jess.

She let out another giggle and closed the door behind her.

CHAPTER 3

Sam dropped into his desk chair. "What the hell is so important, Frank?"

Frank Romano, Sam's longtime partner, was munching on a doughnut and drinking coffee. With his feet on the desk and a deep yawn, he asked, "Who's the new special friend?"

Sam wished he could be as relaxed as Frank whose joking around meant he approved of Sam's finally getting a life again. He had been in the midst of a relationship dry spell. Had a problem with comparing the new ladies with his late wife who, in his mind, had become more perfect as time wore on.

"My friend's none of your freakin' business. This better be good, Frank."

"Jeeze, cool it, buddy. We've got a murder on our hands!"

"When did it happen?"

"Probably last night. They found him in the parking garage on Pelham Avenue, next to the construction company."

"Did he work there?"

"Maybe. Not too many people park there on Saturdays. He wasn't found 'til this afternoon."

Sam stood up, walked over to the coffee table and poured himself a cup. "Where's the body now?"

"At the morgue after the examiner finished."

"Let's go see where it happened."

***

Frank drove. Sam lowered the window, breathing in the smell of the orange groves they passed. He never tired of the beauty of Sarasota. Not paradise, but close. It helped him deal with life's ugly side.

They approached the crime scene. People were gathered outside the garage, and Sam told the patrolman on duty, "Get these people out of here. There's nothing to see."

When he ducked under the barrier tape surrounding the scene, Sam saw a car with a large blood stain on the floor next to it. "Are the forensic people done?"

"They are. It's all yours."

While Sam surveyed the chalked figure and car, he took a package of gum out of his pocket, took a piece, unwrapped it and popped it into his mouth. He opened the car door, searched the back seat and found nothing. Then he opened the glove compartment, "What's this? I think he had a kid."

Sam smoothed out a crumpled child's drawing. It seemed to be a picture of Mickey Mouse together with a mother, father and little boy. "This is pretty good. I wonder how old he is. Why is it crumpled up and thrown in here? I'd hang it up someplace. Has the family been notified?"

"Not yet. Waiting for you."

"Let's do it now."

***

They visited the victim's house located in the better part of town. A typical Florida home; manicured lawn, trimmed shrubs and a basketball hoop in the driveway. Sam walked to the side of the house and saw a pool in the back.

Sam knocked. An attractive woman wearing a bathrobe opened the door. "Who are you?"

The partners showed her their IDs, "We're police detectives. I'm Sam Wesley, and this is Frank Romano. Are you Mrs. Henry Dobson?"

"Yes. What's wrong?"

"Ma'am I'm afraid we have some bad news about your husband."

"Oh no!" Sam caught her as her knees started to buckle, and both men helped her into the living room where they sat down. Sam felt out of place on the elegant couch. He scanned the room. A white rug, light-colored furniture and expensive accessories. Looks like new. The family probably doesn't use it much.

"Mrs. Dobson, your husband was involved in a

shooting."

"Is he all right? What happened?"

"I'm sorry. He didn't make it. From what we can tell, he died instantly."

She rubbed her temples and took a deep breath. "I don't understand."

"We believe it happened last night in the parking garage. When did you see your husband last?"

She pushed to the edge of her seat, the color gone from her face. "Friday morning when he went to work."

"Weren't you wondering why he didn't come home last night?"

She shrugged and shook her head. "No, he had a business trip and told me he'd be taking a plane to Atlanta after work. I didn't expect him back until Sunday."

A young boy watched from the foyer. Sam said, "Let me get you some water, Mrs. Dobson. Frank, I'll be right back."

Sam found the kitchen, and the boy followed him. The kid had a cast on his arm and big frightened eyes. He turned on the faucet. "Hi. My name is Sam. What's yours?"

"Jerry."

"I'm getting water for your mother, Jerry. Don't be scared."

"I'm not, you're a policeman. Why aren't you wearin' a uniform?"

"A detective doesn't have to wear one. But I have

a badge. Sam held his badge out for Jerry to see. "Say, what happened to your arm, Jerry?"

The kid shifted from foot to foot. "I broke it when I fell down the stairs."

"Who put that great cast on you?

"Dr. Arenstein."

"Does it hurt?

"A little. It hurt bad when it happened. But now it feels okay."

"Are you gonna get autographs on the cast?"

Still shifting the boy said, "Nah. I don't think so."

"Why don't we go talk to your mom?"

When Sam and Jerry entered the living room, Frank was trying to calm Mrs. Dobson. Jerry ran to her. She hugged him, kissed his head and said, "Jerry, something terrible happened to Daddy."

"What?"

Mrs. Dobson rubbed Jerry's back. "Your father had a bad accident."

"An accident?"

"Yes, a very bad person shot him."

"Jerry looked confused. "With a gun? Like the movies?"

Mrs. Dobson rubbed her son's back. "Yes, but this isn't the movies, sweetheart. It's real."

The boy shook his head. "Who shot him?"

Mrs. Dobson kissed Jerry on the forehead and took hold of both his hands. "We don't know darling. That's why these two nice detectives are here. They're trying to find out."

"You mean he won't come home anymore?"

"No darling. Your father is in heaven."

Jerry shook his head and crinkled his nose. "Is Daddy dead?"

Mrs. Dobson pulled Jerry toward her and hugged him. "Yes, honey, he is."

Neither Mrs. Dobson nor Jerry cried. After she released him, Jerry resumed shifting both feet and Mrs. Dobson continued to tighten the belt on her robe.

Sam handed her the glass of water. "Is there anyone we can call to come over?"

"Yes, my sister. She lives down the street."

After Mrs. Dobson's sister was called, Jerry said, "I have to go to the bathroom," and he ran out of the room.

Mrs. Dobson asked, "Do you have any idea who's responsible?"

"Not at the moment, but we're just starting our investigation."

She walked around the room, keeping her fingers busy with her robe belt. Sam wanted to delay asking her questions until she calmed down a bit. When her sister came through the door out of breath, she gave Mrs. Dobson a hug and said. "What happened?"

"Oh, Janice. Henry was killed!"

"Killed? Oh my God!"

Mrs. Dobson introduced Janice to the detectives and Sam said, "I need to ask you a few routine questions, Mrs. Dobson. Are you up to it now?"

She rocked from side to side. "Yes, I think so."

Jerry returned and Sam said, "Why doesn't your sister keep Jerry busy in another room."

Jerry's aunt took his hand. He turned his head and kept his eyes glued on Sam.

"Did your husband have any enemies?"

"No, I don't think so." Her manicured fingers were drumming on the side table.

"Where did he work and what did he do?"

"An architect for the Pelham Construction Company."

"Do you know the people he worked with?"

She shrugged, "Some of them."

Sam saw Jerry in the next room. His aunt tried to get his attention, but Jerry continued to watch Sam and his mother.

"Did you and your husband have a happy marriage?"

Mrs. Dobson put her water glass down on the table, got up, walked around the room and rearranged a displayed candy dish and two candle holders. Then, she sat down, swinging her crossed leg back and forth. "Yes, most of the time. All marriages have their ups and downs but he loved me very much."

Sam tried a different approach. "Jerry's a terrific kid."

"Oh! He's my pride and joy."

"Does he like school?"

"Oh yes. He's very smart and loves to draw. He's good at it. When the three of us came back from Disneyworld, he drew a few pictures of us with Mickey Mouse and the other characters there." She beamed, "They were very good if I say so myself."

"I saw one of those drawings. You're right. He's good. I found it in the glove compartment of your husband's car."

"Really?"

Sam stood up, went to the window and looked out. "What happened to Jerry's arm?"

She rubbed the back of her neck. "He broke it. You know kids. Fell off his bike."

Hmm. Why did Jerry tell me he fell down the stairs?

"Did Jerry and your husband spend a lot of time together?"

"I wouldn't say a lot. Henry traveled out of town quite a bit. Worked hard. He was so tired when he got home, he'd often go to bed early."

Sam couldn't believe this guy. Too stupid to be a father. "Did he shoot hoops with Jerry sometimes or play catch?"

"No, but we had a great time in Disneyworld."

Sam nodded. "Again, I'm sorry for your loss. If there's anything else you can think of, please call."

Sam waved to the boy and his aunt. "So long, Jerry."

In the car, Sam said, "Something's screwy here. Get in touch with Dr. Arenstein. He's probably at

Memorial Hospital. Find out about the kid's broken arm.

"Anything else?"

"Yeah. Let's go to the office of the Pelham Construction Company to find out more about Henry.

"When? They're closed 'til Monday."

"On Monday morning bright and early. We'll surprise them.

CHAPTER 4

Jessica's alarm went off at 9 a.m. on Sunday. She had an empty feeling again. Ever since her divorce, she asked the same questions every morning. Why did he screw around on me? Why do I still have regrets? Should I have given him just one more chance?

Today she tried to think of Sam and be optimistic. But couldn't shake the fear that he'd turn out like Steve. Would she ever be able to trust any man?

After she rolled over on her back and allowed herself the luxury of thinking the good things about him, she got up, did a few stretching exercises and made her bed. She put the coffee on and called her partner.

Jess loved to hear the Events greeting. "Good morning, you've reached Event Services. This is Brenda, may I help you?"

After her divorce proceedings, with her self-confidence at a record low, Jess decided to change her life. She gave her notice at work and called her friend. Brenda had been begging Jess to go into business with her. They started Event Services and tackled events from very small to very large. Their hard work paid off. Word spread and the company's still growing.

How are you doing, Bren? Do you need any help?"

"Very funny. I think I can handle a children's birthday party, even though it's for 150 screaming kids. The team is all here and we're okay. Enjoy your day off."

"Thanks, I'll see you tomorrow."

Then Jess called Sara. "Hi, are you up for shopping today? There's a sale at Macy's."

"I'd love it."

"I need to get dressed but should be down to get you at around 10:30. Okay?"

"Perfect. See you then. Don't forget to wear comfortable shoes."

Sara Janus, a new friend, lives on the first floor of the building. Though she's older than Jess, it doesn't matter. They enjoy spending time together.

Jess showered and put on a pair of slacks, a sweater and flat shoes. She brushed her reddish-brown hair, moved her head around and approved of the new style. She applied her makeup and groaned. I wish my freckles would disappear.

Her dates with Sam were hits—even though the last one ended early. The tingle of excitement when she thought about him became even more pronounced when she saw him. Face it, Jessica, the guy's damn sexy.

Today should be fun. Sara's good company. Jess thought of her mother whenever she and Sara talked. Always said the right things to make Jess feel better.

After she downed a cup of coffee, she took the stairs down to Sara's condo. Mark, Sara's son, greeted Jess at the door.

Surprised to see him, Jess said, "Hi Mark, how are you? What are you doing here?"

"I jjjust cccame down to have breakfast with Mmom. She's getting rready. C'mon to the kitchen and have a ccup of ccoffee while you wait."

Mark's speech impediment was more obvious today. "Okay, another cup would be nice."

They talked in the kitchen. Jess thought Brenda would be attracted to Mark. Shy but great looking. Very appealing. She wondered if he had a girlfriend. If not, she planned to introduce them.

Jess's condo is right under Mark's and she'd been bothered by all the noise his shower made. "Say Mark, do you want the name of my plumber?"

"You're sick of all that racket? I know, I am too. I've already called a plumber. He'll be here the middle of next week. Bet you'll miss the noise when it's fixed."

Jess wondered, why no stutter this time?

Sara came into the room and was out of breath.

"Whew! I never dressed so fast. Mark and I talked so much I lost track of time."

"Are you ready, Sara?"

Sara always wore a skirt. No wonder. She had great legs. Working out paid off for her. "Yup, let's go."

Jess started to drive toward the mall. "Why are you staring?"

"Your hair looks great. What did you do?"

"I had it cut. It got too long and kinky. Too much trouble to take care of."

"It brings out your eyes. You know, you're a very pretty girl?"

Jess blushed. "Ya, ya, ya. I belong in Hollywood."

"No, but you do have a glow about you. It must be a guy. Am I right?"

"Sort of. I'm dating someone, but it's too soon to talk about it. Don't want to jinx it."

"I thought so. Sorry it's too late for Mark. Wishful thinking on my part."

Jess drove into a parking space. "There's a shoe sale at Macy's. Let's start there."

They tried on shoes but didn't buy any. Jess almost bought a pair of dressy heels. She fell in love with them, but they were a half size too small.

Jess said, "I don't care. They're almost my size and they're so gorgeous!"

She wore them as she limped over to the cash register. Sara stopped her. "Are you crazy, they'll cripple you." And forced her to take them off.

They went to a different department, tried on and bought a few things. Then agreed to take a break and have lunch.

They waited in line for a while talking about the delicious foods displayed. Usually, Jess's mouth would have watered, but today, no appetite. Could it be love? They searched through the oversized deli menu and both ordered a salad and coffee.

Jess said, "About Mark, he must have a lot of girls chasing him."

"As a matter of fact, he does. I don't know any of them. Mark tells me I'm too nosey."

"Does he like living in Florida?"

"I think so. He wanted to leave the bad memories of Chicago. After his father died, he went through a bad time."

The waitress came by and filled their coffee cups.

"How old was Mark?"

Sara handed her the dish of creamers. "Ten years old and very bright. I worked as a medical secretary and we did okay. With the help of scholarships, Mark graduated college with honors.

"What did he major in?"

"Computer Science. Got a good job. They opened a branch in Florida and wanted him to transfer.

"You didn't come down right away, though."

"No, but I hated the cold weather up there so much, I followed him and here we both are."

Sara excused herself and went to the restroom. Jess admired her figure. Pretty good for a woman her age. I hope I'll be as trim when I get there.

"When Sara returned, Jess asked, "There's someone I want Mark to meet. Do you think he'd mind? She's very intelligent and pretty. Of course, I'm prejudiced; she's one of my best friends."

"I don't know. Ask him and see."

"Okay. Now, an important question. Will we have dessert?"

"Are you kidding? Of course." Jess always had room for sweets, so they shared a gooey dessert, finished shopping and were too tired to talk much on the way home. When Jess drove up to the building, they saw Mark out front. Sara jumped out of the car. "What is it, Mark?"

"Oh, it's the dddarned ppplumbing ththing. Now, there's a bbbad leak ffrom the water heater. I called the pplumber again and he said it would ccost more but he'd ccome today and fix it or replace it. He's going to try and fffix the shower at the sssame tttime."

"So, why are you out here?" Sara asked.

"I just wanted to mmmake sure he'd go to the right condo."

When the plumber showed up, the four of them took the elevator. Jess observed Mark. He's very distraught. All because of a plumbing problem? Strange.

The incident went out of her mind as she rushed down the hall to unlock the door and answer her ringing phone.

CHAPTER 5

Sam got home at 6 o'clock Sunday morning and fell into bed on top of the covers wearing only his shorts. He slept until 3 p.m. He woke up to the sound of a Florida downpour and climbed under the blanket.

I feel like having chicken soup. Yeah, some comfort food would hit the spot.

He got up, put the coffee on and took a quick shower. While he sipped the caffeine, he peered into the fridge. I'll defrost the chicken stored in the freezer, and I've got celery, carrots, onion, parsnips, and the two ingredients for a superb soup: my own special seasonings and a bay leaf. Ought to market it and call it, Superb Soup. Catchy.

Sam prepared the chicken and veggies, put them all in a large pot and started to fill it with water.

Something strange about the kid. It's obvious he and his mother both tried to cover up how the arm got broken. And what kind of father would ignore his child the way he did? What a jerk!

He mixed up all the matzoh ball ingredients. After rolling perfect balls, he placed them on a cookie sheet and put them in the fridge to wait.

Questioning Henry's co-workers will prove interesting. We need to find out more about the guy.

He called ballistics while the soup simmered. And they told him a 38 revolver killed Dobson. Then he gave into an impulse and called Jess.

"Hello. Aaaaa' choo!!" Jess answered out of breath and with a sneeze.

"What kind of greeting is that?"

"I may have the start of a little cold. I thought you were working."

"I worked on a case all night, came home, got some sleep and made chicken soup. I miss you. Tell me about your day with Sara?"

"She's fun. We just got back and I'm about to try all my stuff on to make sure everything fits. A busy day. How'd your case go?"

"A challenge, but I don't want to talk about work. What I do want is to see you before next Saturday. How about tonight? We could share a bowl of soup."

"Could you bring it here? I'm beat and want to get comfortable."

With his cell wedged between his ear and shoulder, Sam got some containers out of the pantry. "I could and my soup will cure your cold. I'll leave as soon as it's ready. Should be there in a couple hours."

"Good, it'll give me some time to straighten up this mess."

Sam sat at his desk and went over his notes. Breathed in the aroma of the pot on the stove. For the first time since his wife died, he felt happy; his job going well and crazy about Jess.

He strained the soup, put it back on the stove, carefully dropped the matzoh balls into the bubbling broth, and wondered about Dobson's family. The wife appeared to be upset, but he didn't think she really gave a shit. And how did the boy fit in? He's a nice kid, but something's off there.

After everything cooled, he poured it all into a large container. As his mother used to say, "A bowl of health."

Before going to Jess's, Sam had enough time to make some calls and do an errand. After checking a few stores nearby and asking whether they carried the brand of Jess's shoes, he put her broken-heeled pair in a shopping bag, packed the food in insulated containers and drove to the mall. He found the right store and spoke to the woman in charge of the shoe department.

"I think these shoes are defective. My girlfriend wore them once and look what happened." He was surprised she replaced them without an argument. Must be my charm. Jess'll be ecstatic. I can't wait to see the look on her face.

At Jess's door, he took her all in. She scrubbed

her face clean of makeup, had a jogging suit on and socks on her feet. She looked great and rose on her tiptoes to kiss him on the cheek. She took some of his packages, and they brought the food into the kitchen. He felt the warm atmosphere of her place. Always fresh flowers in the foyer and the dining room. I could get used to this.

He unpacked and handed her a package. "How did this get in here?"

Jess opened it, jumped up and down and hugged him. She put the shoes on and wore them while they ate.

Sam said, "I don't think they match your sweat suit and socks."

"I don't care."

They sat at the kitchen table. "Is your cold better yet?"

Jess gulped spoonfuls of soup. "I think so but I'm not quite sure. Can I have some more?"

"I suppose, but remember, you owe me."

"Are we still on for next Saturday?"

"Of course."

"I've been thinking. Instead of going out, how about my having a small dinner party?"

"Good idea, how small?"

Jess lit up. "Six people including us. I'll invite Sara, Mark and my partner, Brenda. It'll be a good way to introduce her to Mark. Also, I'll ask Richard Benson, my next-door neighbor. What do you think?"

An encouraging sign. She must want to show me off. "I'll provide the main dish."

"You're on."

"How about veal parmesan? And I'll bring dessert too—maybe tiramisu. You can make everything else."

"It's a plan."

When the doorbell sounded, she went to answer it, and came back to the kitchen with an older, handsome man. "Sam Wesley, meet Richard Benson. He's one of my favorite neighbors."

Sam felt a ping of jealousy. I hope this guy isn't my competition. Nah, he's too old. But still, stranger things have happened. I'm gonna have to fix that. They shook hands.

Richard said, "Oh I'm sorry, I interrupted your dinner."

"Not at all. How about joining us?"

"Thanks, but I've already eaten. I have a question, Jess."

"What's up?"

"If you're going to be at the condo meeting next Tuesday, could you submit a list of complaints to the Board? I'll be out of town for a couple of days to visit my son."

"Of course. Oh, and I have a question for you. I'm having a small dinner party next Saturday. Will you come?"

"Sure. Sounds like fun. Can I bring something?"

"Nope, just your handsome self."

31

Richard blushed, "Okay. Now finish your dinner. I have some packing to do. Good to meet you, Sam."

After Richard left and they went back to eating, Sam pushed a lock of hair out of her eyes. "He seems nice."

Jess held her feet out and admired her shoes. "He is. Bought his place last year. He worked for a large law firm in Rhode Island. He and his wife planned to move down together. When she died, he came anyway. He's interesting to talk to."

Sam grabbed one of her legs and put it in his lap. "Should I be jealous?"

"Maybe. You know I'm attracted to older men."

"How about giving this old man a kiss?"

"Are you willing to risk catching my maybe cold?"

He flashed his winning smile. "Yes."

Sam stood up, pulled her out of the chair and kissed her, and kissed her, and kissed her while they backed into the bedroom.

***

Early the next morning, he got out of bed without making a sound, kissed Jess on the forehead, took a moment to watch her sleep and brushed a few stray hairs away from her eyes. How did I get so lucky?

He got dressed and went into the kitchen to make coffee. He poured two cups and brought one to Jess, leaving it on the night table with a note. "Good morning, Jessica. Sadly, I have to go and

catch the bad guys. I'll call you tonight—Very affectionately, Sam."

CHAPTER 6

When Sam met Frank at the Pelham Construction Company, people were just coming to work. They checked in with the security guard at the front desk who called the manager of Henry Dobson's department. They were directed to his office. The manager stood up and extended his hand. "I'm Jim Spencer, how can I help you gentlemen?"

They shook hands and introduced themselves. Sam asked, "Have you heard about Henry Dobson's murder last Friday?

"I did."

Frank sneezed. His allergy bothered him again. "We need to see his office."

Spencer shook his head. "It's unbelievable. I still can't get over it. Come with me and I'll show you where he sat. Henry was a terrific architect. I'll miss him."

They opened drawers and checked file cabinets.

The dusty office, dead plants and crammed files created a weird odor. Frank kept sneezing and blowing. He said, "Jeeze, I hope we can get out of here soon. I'm dying."

A tall red-headed man, wearing a plaid jacket and sporting a mustache stood in the doorway and asked, "Can I help you, gentlemen?"

Sam said, "We're the detectives investigating the murder of Henry Dobson. What's your name?"

"Mac Standish. My cubicle is next door. What an awful thing. We talked just last Friday. He must have died a short time afterward. What happened?"

"On the way to his car in the parking garage, someone shot him. Did you know him well?"

"I guess. We've known each other for a while."

"Would you have any idea who'd want to do this?"

He leaned against the wall and kept throwing a pencil in the air. "No, I don't. People seemed to like him; a little impressed with himself, but I don't think that would be a reason for anyone to kill him."

Sam said, "He died Friday. When I spoke to his wife, she said she wasn't surprised he didn't come home that night. Had to go out of town on business. Do you know anything about that?"

"I do. He didn't go out of town and had no business. He had plans to meet a woman. Had an eye for the ladies. I don't think his wife knew about it, but who knows?"

Standish couldn't wait to trash the guy.

Sam asked, "Do you know the woman?"

"Yes. She works here, so I'd rather not say who it is."

This guy's a typical office busybody. Probably spends most of his time listening to people's conversations. Sam said, "I'm afraid you'll have to. This is a murder investigation."

"Okay, but please don't tell anyone else if you can help it. I don't want her to get into trouble. Her name is Pamela Offerson, one of our salespeople. She sits three cubicles down."

Sam didn't think the guy really gave a rat's ass if she'd get in trouble. "Thanks." He turned to Frank. "Let's visit Miss Offerson."

They strolled down to her office and saw a fairly attractive dark-haired, buxom woman, with glasses. She was punching numbers on a calculator. Sam said, "Hi, Pamela Offerson?"

"Yes."

The two detectives introduced themselves. Sam asked, "When did you last see Henry Dobson?"

After she examined her calculator printout, she said, "I guess Friday here at the office. We were supposed to meet in the cocktail lounge at the Colby Hotel but he never showed. I thought he stood me up, so I went home."

Sam asked, "Were you with anyone at home?"

"Yes. My roommate, Sheila.

"How well did you know Dobson?"

She removed her glasses and her deep-set eyes

were more obvious. Sam didn't think she was half as attractive as Dobson's wife. Some men are never satisfied.

"Detective, can you keep what I tell you confidential?'

She lowered her voice and motioned for them to sit by her desk. Sam said, "I'll try to, but I can't promise."

"We've been seeing each other socially. We were physically attracted to each other is all. We had no future. He made me feel beautiful and important, so I kept dating him."

"Did he talk to you about his marriage or his child?"

"Not about his marriage, but he complained about his son, Jerry. I guess the boy has a behavior problem and Henry had to be super-strict with him."

Sam and Frank nodded to each other. Sam said, "What do you mean by super-strict."

"He would take away some of his privileges and sometimes he hit him in order to straighten him out. Nothing severe, mind you, but just a tap to keep him in line."

"Do you know his wife?"

"Slightly."

"Did you know if he hit his wife too?"

"No. He didn't mention it."

"OK thank you, Miss Offerson. We'll let you know if we need anything else."

They agreed Pamela Offerson probably told the truth but would check the alibi she gave them anyway to rule her out as a suspect.

"Frank, it's lunchtime. I'm gonna stop by my apartment and have a bowl of my Superb Soup. Will you join me?"

"No thanks. I'll catch up with you later. Do you want to nose around the Dobsons' neighborhood this afternoon?"

"Yeah. I'll meet you in front of their house at about two."

After lunch Sam stopped by the station to speak to Jim Seavey, his supervisor.

Sam liked Jim. They respected each other. Before Jim started, Sam was offered that job, but refused it. He didn't want to be stuck behind a desk. Sam asked, "What's shakin', boss?"

"You seem chipper today. What's going on?"

Sam didn't hesitate to say, "Our victim was a philanderer and a child-beater. I'm beginning to think he deserved to die. Have you reached the child's doctor yet?"

"Yup. The doctor told me his broken arm could have been an accident, but probably is the result of a beating. He said there were black and blue marks all over the kid's body."

"Son of a bitch. He did deserve to die.

CHAPTER 7

Jess woke up to the wafting aroma of morning coffee and a note propped up against a covered coffee cup.

"Very affectionately!" What does that mean? After last night, couldn't he be a little more personal? He sure didn't hold back then. But, coffee's a nice touch. Maybe it's too soon to say everything. She reached over and called Brenda.

"Event Services, this is Brenda. May I help you?

"Bren, it's me. Sorry, but I had a late night and overslept. I'll get there as soon as I can."

"A late night, huh? What were you doing?"

Jess knew she meant well, but she didn't want to talk about Sam yet. Too new. "See you soon."

After she hung up, Jess called Sara. "Hello."

"Hi Sara, it's Jess. Do you have a few minutes?"

"I'm just about to leave for work, but always have time for you, Sweetie."

"Good. Listen, I've decided to have a small dinner party next Saturday night. Can you and Mark come?"

"I will. But I can't speak for Mark."

"I'll ask him. Talk to you soon."

After Jess got dressed, she stopped by Mark's condo. He opened the door before she had a chance to ring his bell. "Hi. I have a question."

"Shoot."

"Will you come to my dinner party Saturday night? It'll be a small group and I think you'll enjoy yourself"

"Ththanks. I'll be there. What time?"

"Come around seven o'clock and you can dress casual."

Jess knew Brenda would go for Mark. He's gorgeous.

"Ggreat. See you then. I'm just off to work. Are you ggoing down?"

`As they were leaving the building, Jess asked, "Did you get the flood fixed?"

"Yes, and nno more shower noise. Are you happy?"

"You got that right. I won't miss it."

They waved and got into their cars.

***

Jess felt proud every time she stepped into the Event Services office. She and Brenda decorated it as though it were a comfortable room at home. Cookies and candy on the coffee table, coffee and china cups on the small server and vases of flowers on each desk. She still couldn't believe they made this thing work. Of course, the right partnership had everything to do with it. They were on the same wavelength and though their personalities were different, they understood and respected each other.

"Brenda, I've arrived."

"So I see. Tell me. What kept you up last night?"

Today, as usual, Brenda wore high heels. Her black slacks and top were set off by her blond hair and striking gold jewelry. Quite sophisticated. Compared to Jess's freckle-faced outdoor look, Brenda exuded glamour.

"Never mind last night. I have something more important to talk about. Since we don't have anything on the books next Saturday, I'm having a dinner party and I want you to come."

"How come? You don't cook, remember?"

"I won't be doing all the cooking. Sam is bringing the main course and the dessert."

"Oh? Tell me more."

Jess walked over to the cookies and took one. After tasting it, she nodded her head in approval.

"One of the other guests will be a young handsome neighbor I want you to meet. Mark Janus. I know you'll like him. He's hot."

"You know how I feel about blind dates."

"It isn't a blind date. He's just one of the other guests. If you don't care for him, you don't have to pay any attention to him."

"Can I bring something?"

"Maybe some wine. We're having veal."

Jess finished her cookie. She stretched her arms and yawned, remembering last night. Sam was great. Now she knew what he meant when he said he gets better.

"Getting back to Sam, why are you so tired? Come clean."

"Bren, I may be hooked. Even his little faults don't annoy me."

"Really?"

"Anyway, it's too soon to talk about anything."

"I understand. Now, let's talk about the big wedding we have booked and the cocktail party tomorrow night."

"Good. Business as usual will keep me focused."

They continued to plan for future bookings and spent the day updating their schedule. In the middle of discussing the pros and cons of having their next wedding event take place outside or inside, the phone rang.

"Event Services, this is Jess. How may I help you?"

"You can have a cup of coffee with me, so I can see you and use you as a sounding board."

Jess's stomach fluttered. "Who may I ask is calling?"

"A not-so-secret admirer."

"Sam, we just saw each other last night."

"We did? It seems longer. No kidding, can you carve some time out for me?"

She toyed with the idea of saying no. He might start taking me for granted. Maybe I should play a little hard to get. Oh, what the hell.

"Of course. I can meet you at the diner across the street in, say, 15 minutes. We can have dinner. I'm just about done here."

"Okay, see you in 15."

Brenda looked at Jess. "I'm not saying a word."

"Good."

Jess grabbed her bag and left.

She took a booth and spotted Sam coming in the door limping down to sit with her. I love his gorgeous smile and the way his face lights up when he sees me. I'm happy I didn't play hard to get. It's a stupid game. "Your leg bothering you today?"

"A little. An extra-strength aspirin will fix me up." He popped it in his mouth and washed it down with some of the water put out for him. "All better."

"What's new?"

They were holding hands across the table.

"This will be hypothetical, because I wouldn't discuss anything specific about my case, right?"

Jess was excited. Sam wanted to confide in her. "Right."

"Suppose a ladies man murdered on the way to meeting his latest girlfriend also had a wife and child who had a cast on his arm. The child says he fell down some stairs and on separate questioning, the wife says he broke it after falling off his bike.

What would be your impression?"

Jess thought carefully before answering. "They're both covering up the cause of the injury."

Sam drew her hand to his mouth and kissed it.

"I thought so too, so we contacted the kid's doctor and he said it could've been a fall from his bike, but there were black and blue marks all over the boy. So he concluded the break may have been connected to a beating."

Jess was really getting into this stuff. "What does this have to do with the father's murder? How old is the boy?"

He pushed back a lock of her hair. "The boy is only 9 years old."

"The wife?"

"Could be. I'm going back to question her again tomorrow."

"What about the girlfriend? Did you speak to her?"

"I wondered about her too. I think we'll talk to her again."

"Sam, you're full of it. You thought all the same things.'

"I know, but it's nice talking to you about it and an excuse to see you again so soon."

"You don't need an excuse." Jess smiled and reached over the table to kiss him.

CHAPTER 8

After they met in front of the Dobson house, Frank started questioning people living across the street while Sam interviewed the next-door neighbor.

Sam rang the bell. This house and the Dobson's were the same. It struck him how similar most Florida houses were. Beautiful, but he thought if he had a house, it would be cozier—more like New England—wooden shingles instead of stucco. Why the sudden interest in real estate? Sam knew the answer. He imagined Jess living in his house.

The neighbor said, "Yes, can I help you?"

He introduced himself and asked if he could speak to her about Henry Dobson.

She said, "Of course."

She wore glasses, had a friendly face and wore a sweat suit. Must have been jogging. "How well did you know the Dobsons?"

"We nodded when we saw each other, and I spoke

to Mrs. Dobson now and then. I think she wanted to be a friend, but I got the impression her husband didn't."

"Do you have any children?"

"Yes, we have a 10-year-old girl. Why?"

"Does she know Jerry?"

"They go to the same school and sometimes sit together on the bus."

"Did he stay out of school a lot?"

"No. But one time she did mention Jerry stayed home for a few days. When she saw him next, he had a patch over one eye."

While they were talking, Sam's eyes drifted toward the kitchen and saw a bunch of a kid's papers and drawings displayed on the fridge. Unlike the Dobson's refrigerator—nothing displayed there. Mr. Dobson probably didn't want to see them.

"Did Jerry tell her why he wore a patch?"

"He said he had an accident and didn't want to talk about it. I thought it strange at the time."

Sam hated to think the bastard used Jerry as a punching bag. He's such a nice kid.

She went on to say Jerry always hung back whenever she saw the three of them and never saw the father and son alone together.

He thanked her and met up with Frank again. "I think I'm going to revisit Mrs. Dobson. Could you go back to Pam Offerson, the girlfriend at Pelham Construction? See if she really went home after Dobson stood her up."

***

Jerry answered the door and Sam said, "Hello again. Is your mom home?"

"Not right now, we ran out of milk. She'll be here pretty soon."

"Can I come in?"

"I guess it's all right."

"How's your arm feeling?"

"A lot better. I hope I won't have to keep this cast on too long."

"Jerry, I guess you'll miss doing stuff with your dad."

Jerry looked off to the side. "No, we didn't do much. I used to get him mad all the time."

Mrs. Dobson motioned Sam to go into the kitchen with her and she started putting the groceries away.

Sam asked, "Did your husband hit Jerry?"

"No."

"Mrs. Dobson, I got two different answers when I asked how he broke his arm."

Mrs. Dobson said, "I got two incidents mixed up."

"Oh, was there another time he broke his arm?"

"Not his arm, but he did have a fractured ankle. That's what mixed me up."

Sam said, "I'm not surprised. His doctor told us the black and blue marks on his body indicated he had been beaten more than once. So, I have to conclude you're not telling me the truth. How did Jerry really break his arm?"

They both took a chair at the kitchen table, and she started to cry. When she spoke again her voice shook. "He couldn't help himself. I tried so hard to stop him, but I couldn't. No matter what Jerry did or said, he'd go into a rage."

"Who?"

"My husband."

"Why didn't you call the police?"

Still crying she said, "I know I should have but kept thinking he'd do something worse if I did."

Sam gave her his handkerchief. "Mrs. Dobson, did you know your husband had an affair?"

"I suspected as much, but I couldn't be sure."

"Why didn't you just take Jerry and leave him?"

"Believe me, I thought about it a lot, but I have no money in my name and my family wouldn't be able to help me. If he ever found out I planned to leave him, he would have killed me—or worse, Jerry."

The poor woman. She had a motive all right and was a viable suspect. But Sam saw her desperate situation and wouldn't have blamed her.

"Where were you Friday evening?

"Here at home."

"Did you see or talk to anyone?"

"Just Jerry, we were playing Monopoly."

"Mrs. Dobson, do you own a gun?"

She started crying again, walked over to the counter, tore off a paper towel and blew her nose.

"Mr. Wesley, sure, I'm glad he's dead, but I didn't kill him."

"I'm asking you again. Do you own a gun?"

She started to sob harder and shook her head. Her eyes were red and her face puffy. "It's my husband's. He bought it for protection."

"May I borrow it?"

"Do I need a lawyer?"

"You can call one if you want to."

"Yes, I do."

"Call him. Tell him to meet us down at the station. We'll finish questioning you there."

"Am I under arrest or anything?"

"No, we just have to clear up a few things."

She called her lawyer, and both she and Jerry got into Sam's car.

CHAPTER 9

In Jess's kitchen, Sam completed finishing touches to the food. Dressing in her bedroom, she breathed in the aromas and sighed. I can't believe my luck. A macho guy and he cooks too!

She pulled the new dress over her head happy about the color she chose. Blue, Sam's favorite. Matched her condo too. Bending over to see the vanity mirror, she made a face and dabbed some concealer on an unwelcome zit. Then patted her hair—thank goodness, no trace of frizz.

She entered the kitchen, and Sam didn't stop working, but raised his face to her and puckered his lips for a kiss. "Hi, beautiful."

"Hi yourself. Smells delicious. How can I help you?"

"Everything's under control, but thanks anyway."

She checked the table, rearranged the centerpiece and walked through the rooms to make sure they looked perfect.

Brenda, her first guest, arrived while Jess was putting out the hors d'oeuvres. She handed Jess a couple of bottles of wine. "Hi, partner."

Brenda looked sensational. She wore a simple white dress that showed off her great figure.

"Bren, come, I want you to meet Sam." Jess pulled her into the kitchen.

He was creating a little assembly line of food and looked up. "You must be Brenda."

"It's a pleasure to meet you, Sam. Boy, are you efficient."

"Yup, I'm showing off to Jess. If I need a second job someday, you might want to hire me."

Jess signed, "Don't tempt us. We better get out of your way so you can hurry up and join us."

The doorbell rang again. Sara and Mark arrived. "Sara and Mark Janus, this is Brenda Magrini.

"Hi, it's nice to meet you." When Brenda saw Mark, she raised her eyebrows. They exchanged smiles.

After Richard Benson arrived with a bunch of flowers and Jess introduced him, she offered drinks and passed the hors d'oeuvres. It was an amenable group and Mark, more at ease than usual, didn't stammer.

At the dinner table Mark said, "Brenda, you're a pleasant surprise. Where has Jess been hiding you?"

"Oh, I'm the workhorse in the Events stable. But I do get out once in a while."

"I'm sure you do. We should get together sometime. What do you think?"

"I think it's a great idea."

They arranged a future date and turned their attention to the conversation. Sam was answering questions about his recipes. Then, Mark asked, "Sam, have you had any interesting cases lately?"

"Yeah. As a matter of fact, I'm involved in one now. It's one of the reasons I'm enjoying this evening so much. It's a welcome change."

"Can you share some of the details?"

"It's still a work in progress. But when it's solved, we'll have another dinner party and I'll be able to talk my head off."

"Oh, too bad. I'd love to hear about your typical day. What you do is a hell of a lot more exciting compared to mine. Which is sitting in front of a computer all day. C'mon. Just one clue?"

Jess wondered why Mark couldn't take a hint. Sam tried to smile. "Sorry."

"Fair enough."

Sara changed the subject and asked, "So, Richard, how long have you lived in the building?"

The night flew by. Before the guests left, there were the usual cheek-kissings and hand-shakings and "We have to do this again sometime."

Brenda whispered to Jess, "You're right, he's hot."

When the door finally closed, Sam put his arms around Jess. "You're a wonderful, beautiful hostess. I had fun. Thank you." And kissed her.

"I did too." And she kissed him back. He started

leading her toward the bedroom. Jess asked, "What about the dishes?"

"What about 'em?" Sam answered and muffled her response with another kiss.

***

The dishes waited until the following morning, and they restored the condo to its pre-party condition. We make a great team, Sam thought. He was sure they had a future, but maybe he should cool it for a while. He didn't want to scare her off. Just let nature take its course. On his way home, he made a quick turn and stopped off at the station to see what happened with the Dobson case and met up with Frank.

"What's new with Mrs. Dobson?"

"Well, her lawyer showed up and insisted she didn't have to answer any more questions unless we charged her with something. So she left. I think we should try to get a search warrant to find the gun."

They decided to wait until the next day to get the warrant and went out for a cup of coffee. "How's Jess?" Frank asked.

"Good."

"C'mon tell me more."

"It's too soon, and I don't want to talk about it yet. But I can say she's great."

His mind turned back to the murder. What if the gun didn't prove Mrs. Dobson did it? Where would we go from there? Maybe he should go back to the garage, the scene of the murder. Try harder to find someone who saw something.

Sam didn't find anything new at the scene. On the way out he drove up to the parking attendant in the enclosure. "Hi, I'm Sam Wesley, and I'm investigating the murder on Friday evening. What time did you get off?"

The man examined a notebook hanging on a chain in his booth.

"I worked until 5:30."

"Did you notice anything or anyone unusual."

"No except for a person I didn't recognize. He took the elevator to get his car."

"Can you describe him?"

He paused a moment. "Black and wore thick glasses. Kinda thin. Had one of them baseball caps on."

The attendant stopped to collect money from a departing car.

"Did he speak to you?"

"No, just went to the elevator."

"Did he leave while you were still here?

"No, come to think of it, he didn't."

"Thanks. You've been very helpful."

Sam drove off. Probably nothing, but he'd have to think about it.

CHAPTER 10

In Florida, all the snowbirds descend on the state from November through April. During the busy season, Jess and Sam were swamped with work. Jess with weddings, birthdays, anniversaries and holiday celebrations and Sam with a bunch of nuisance cases. They still made time to be together even for just a cup of coffee.

When things started to ease up, Sam called, "Hi Jess. It's supposed to be hot tomorrow. How about going to the beach?"

"Oh Sam, I'd love it. How did you know I adore the beach?

"You told me."

"Nobody likes a wise ass, Sam. Tomorrow is a slow day for me, so it'll be perfect. I'll pack up a lunch and lots of sunblock."

"Okay. But I'll pack the lunch and you can bring the sunblock. I'll take a beach umbrella too. I don't want us to burn."

"I can feel the sun already. See you tomorrow. Is 10 okay?"

"See you at 10 tomorrow, sweetheart."

***

Jess woke before the alarm went off. Stretched and felt content and happy. Threw off her covers and put on her bathing suit. She got all of her stuff together, sat at the kitchen table and sipped a cup of coffee while she waited for Sam.

She remembered the beach as a kid in Massachusetts. Every Sunday during the summer she and her parents would go. They brought an orange and brown striped blanket and put all the food and drinks on it under the umbrella. Her mom unpacked the food she prepared for lunch and her father sat on a beach chair with his fair skin all covered up. Right after they got there, Jess would run into the water, no matter how cold, until her mother walked to the water's edge and shouted, "Come out and have lunch, Jessica, you're turning blue." The sun and salt air increased her appetite and food tasted so much better there. She loved building sand castles and then destroying them with her feet before running along the shallow water. She'd come home, shower off the gritty sand all over. Hardly able to stay awake while having supper, she'd fall asleep right after she hit the pillow. Those were some of the happiest memories of her childhood.

Sam got there on time. He grabbed Jess's stuff.

"A beautiful Florida day. How about we keep driving and run away from all this?"

"No, I love it here. How about we go to the beach and enjoy all this?"

"You win."

They unpacked and set up the chairs and umbrella and spread the blanket. Both plopped down on their stomachs and sighed at the same time.

Jess said, "The sound of the people around us talking is louder when your head is down. You can eavesdrop and they don't even know it."

"You're a snoop."

"Yeah, I am. She turned on her back. You know, it just dawned on me, this is the place where all five senses are used.

Sam teased her. "My, I didn't know you were such a poet." He tickled her rib cage. Jess pushed him away and started in on him. He laughed so hard it hurt, "Stop, stop, my stomach's killing me."

"Now, you'll remember never to make fun of me. Let's grab a swim. I'm getting hot already."

Sam grabbed Jess, picked her up, ran into the water and dumped her in, "Now you'll remember never to tickle me."

They splashed and ducked each other. Treaded water while they kissed until Sam said, "We better get out of here before I make a spectacle of myself."

They ran back to the blanket, resumed their former stomach position, and after Sam caught his breath, he said, "Jess, I think I love you."

"You think??"

"I'm sure I love you."

"Much better." Jess said.

She stayed quiet. Sam waited but couldn't stand it anymore and repeated "Much better?"

"I love you too, Sam."

They kissed long and sweet and didn't need to say anything else. They dozed off for a while and Jess woke first, "I'm famished. What did you bring us?"

"Sandwiches and iced tea. I don't make gourmet meals all the time."

"Sounds gourmet to me."

Sam opened the basket, took a couple of sandwiches out and poured their drinks. They sat back to back and started eating. Jess said, "Taste's good. Say Sam, how's your murder case going, or should I say your hypothetical murder case?"

"It's at a standstill. We weren't able to get a search warrant for the gun her husband bought. But I don't think the mother did it anyway. She has an alibi."

"What's the alibi?"

"She played Monopoly with her son the night of the murder. I've been keeping busy with a bunch of nuisance cases though."

"What are those?"

"You don't want to know."

"Yes I do."

"They're not very interesting. But you asked for it. There were arrests of shoplifters, DUIs, lewd and lascivious exhibition and disorderly intoxication. Then there were a couple more sophisticated cases, such as an intoxicated man urinating on an arresting officer."

Jess almost choked on her drink. "You're not serious."

"I kid you not. And then my all-time favorites, an accused drunk driver running over himself."

"How?"

Sam then stood up and while he explained, he acted it out. "The man fell from his open car door with the car still running," Sam threw himself on the sand, and said, "both of his legs were run over by the driver's side rear tire. He waved his hands over his legs. "Wanna hear more?"

She heard enough. Jess got a kick out of him. You never knew what he'd say next. She was crazy about him.

They resumed their former position—stomach down—and Sam's arm reached over and it rested on Jess's butt.

"Sam, guess what?" She didn't wait for his answer, "Brenda is dating Mark and Sara's dating Richard."

"Is Richard a grandfather?"

"No, why do you ask?"

"When you first introduced him to me, he said he planned to visit his son, so I thought he had grandchildren."

"His son is in his twenties and is autistic. He lives in a home in North Carolina."

"Why North Carolina?"

"It's a place run by people who are experienced in helping autistic people. Sort of a community. He's been there a long time."

They turned on their sides to face each other and kissed.

Sam asked, "Does he have any other children?"

"No, his wife couldn't have any more, and now his son keeps asking for the mother. Richard tried to tell him she died, but it's hard to get through to him."

"Boy, what a tough break."

"Yuh. And when he told me about his son, he said he felt cheated because he never had a normal kid."

Sam stood and pulled Jess up. "I'm hot again. Let's go cool off."

They ran in, ducked, swam a little and then bobbed up and down together. Sam asked, "And you said Sara's son is seeing Brenda?"

"Uh huh, but she's not talking. Sort of when we started dating. So, it must be getting serious."

"Hey, we better pack up and leave. You didn't re-apply the sunblock and you're getting burned."

"How come you're not?"

"My skin isn't as delicate."

"Such a wonderful day. I love you, Sam. Isn't it nice to say it out loud?"

With a peck on the cheek, Sam said, "Let's go home, honey, so we can say it right.

CHAPTER 11

The Avenger slips into the hospital room and sees a young boy in the midst of a network of tubes. The mechanical cadence of the respirator is deafening. The Avenger stays a while and listens. This confirms a decision and The Avenger slips out and joins a wave of people.

The Voice quieted for a while after the murder of the last victim. Now the excitement and The Voice are back.

The prey is sighted outside the psychiatric department of the hospital. He starts walking and looks backward several times. The Avenger ducks in the shadows and isn't discouraged—just keeps following and biding time.

Though a stately man, the prey hunches over and keeps his head down. Does not see the houses he passes nor the vehicles speeding by. Every so often he rolls his shoulders and head. His walk hastens to a trot. Tries to catch his breath and slows down. Crosses the street without checking to see if anything is coming.

***

Bert Watson walked home from the doctor's office. He had so much on his mind he wondered why his head didn't burst. After Tim collapsed on the football field, he tried to talk to his wife about Tim, but it was too painful. Every day they both sat by their son's hospital bed and didn't speak. The doctors said he had a brain hemorrhage.

He kept going over it in his mind; seeing Tim go down; the coaches running out to him. Thinking maybe he lost his breath for a minute. The trainer coming on the field and getting him up; then Tim falling down again.

Bert started to trot. I'm responsible. I should have let him quit the team after he suffered a concussion last month. But no, I made him go back. I told him not to be afraid. After all, his doctors cleared him.

He started to walk a little slower. I should have watched Tim for signs of a problem and I didn't.

His pace started up again. What do we do now? Send Tim to rehab and visit him there for the rest of his life? The psychiatrist was no help. He had no answers. There were no answers.

He went up his front steps. Bert felt a thud in his back. He reached behind to see why and sunk to his knees. Bert closed his eyes and saw the smiling face of his son, Tim.

CHAPTER 12

"Ooooh, I hurt." Jess cried out while she tried to re-move her bathing suit.

Outside the bathroom door Sam asked, "What is it?"

"I have a baaaaad sunburn."

"I told you to be careful. You were careless, and you didn't listen to me."

He didn't have to scold her. He isn't her father. "Don't yell at me, Sam, I don't like it."

"I'm sorry baby. I just hate for you to suffer."

"I found out what's not so perfect about you."

"What are you talking about?"

"Nothing—Sam, would you mind going to the drugstore to get some of that white stuff?"

"You mean calamine lotion?"

"That's it."

"Do you need anything else?"

"Nope."

"I'm on my way."

Jess put on a pair of panties and walked out of the bathroom with her arms held away from her body. She tried not to let anything touch her and sat down on a kitchen stool.

I feel awful. I think I have a temperature. How could I have been so stupid? Lying out and frying in the Florida sun. What a great day though. Who cares about a sunburn? I hope he doesn't think I only want him because he takes care of me. That's not true. I love Sam because he has everything. Good-natured, sexy, fun and gentle. I want to make him as happy as he makes me.

After he came back, Sam got right to work. "Do you have any vinegar?"

"I think so. It would be in one of the kitchen cabinets."

He opened each cabinet until he found it. Then got a towel and a bowl. He soaked the towel with vinegar and wrung it out. "Let's go to the bedroom and you lie down on your stomach."

Jess held her arms out and walked side to side with her legs apart. She tried to figure out how she could get on her stomach. She lay down and held back a scream. "What are you doing?"

Sam put the compress on her back. "This is a poultice. It'll take a lot of the heat out of the sunburn." He held it down for a while, then moved it to her legs and held it there. "Sit up and let's do your front."

He wrung out the towel again and placed it over

her shoulders, then to her chest and midriff. After he did her thighs and legs, Sam asked, "How does it feel now?"

Jess thought she died and went to heaven? She started to feel good. He had to be crazy about her. She was a mess of dry, red skin. "I smell fishy, but I think it feels better."

He removed the last poultice and patted her dry. "Now, let's apply the calamine."

He applied the lotion and sighed. "Where's your softest top?"

She put on the short nightie he found. "You have a gentle touch. Were you a doctor in your other life?"

"No, just a sunburn victim." He handed the calamine to her. "You can do the face yourself."

"Okay." After she put the lotion on her face she asked, "How do I look?"

"Isn't love blind?"

"Very funny."

He helped her up and took her back to the living room. "What else can I do to make you feel better?"

"I don't know. What do you suggest?"

"A kiss and some food. Pucker up."

Sam landed his lips on hers. He tried not to touch the rest of her face. "Now, the food. What do you want?"

"Scrambled eggs and toast will be just fine, thank you."

He scrambled eggs and popped bread in the toaster. His cell phone sounded the Star Spangled Banner—a work call.

"Hi, Frank."

"We've got another murder. The same M.O. as the Dobson case."

"Dammit!"

"It happened last night in front of the victim's house."

"I'll meet you at the station in about 30 minutes."

He arranged Jess's food on a tray and brought it to her.

"Do you have to leave?"

"Yeah, I'm afraid so. There's been another murder."

They maneuvered a kiss and Sam said, "Maybe you can ask Sara if she wants to keep you company. Get your mind off the burn."

She started to sample her eggs. "I just might. Bye, and don't work too hard. I love you."

He paused for a moment and then in a serious tone. "Me too. Jess, you make me very happy!"

"Because I'm so beautiful?"

Sam flashed his great smile. "Yes. Rest and feel better. Call you later."

***

Sara got up wearing an old housecoat and slippers. It surprised Jess. She never saw Sara in her lounge attire.

Sara said, "Yikes. What happened and what do I

smell?"

"Sam applied vinegar poultices to get the heat out."

"Oh, you should watch it honey, you're so fair."

"Sam already yelled at me, don't start."

Sara plopped down on the couch. "Tell me about your day before you burned to a crisp?

"Wonderful. We're in love. I still can't believe it."

"It's no more than you deserve. Sam's a great guy. I hope he appreciates you."

"I think he does. Tell me what's been going on with you."

Sara cleared her throat. "Been seeing Richard quite a bit. It's been fun. He told me about his son and asked me if I'd want to go with him the next time he visits. But I don't know."

"Why not?"

"It seems too personal. I think he's rushing me a little."

"Just be honest. You could tell him yes but you don't feel it's the right time yet."

"I think I will. You're so wise, Jessica."

"Yes, I am and I also enjoy telling people what to do."

Sara got up and started roaming. "Richard's been good for me. We both understand what it is to be alone, but Mark says to take it slow. I guess he worries. He doesn't want me to be hurt again. You know. Because of his father."

Jess agreed with Mark. Richard seemed to be

moving too fast. "I thought his dad died when Mark was young."

"He did, but there were problems in the marriage. He drank and didn't treat Mark well."

"Does Mark remember?"

At least Jess's ex-husband didn't have a kid to beat up. Just a cheat. She didn't think Sam would ever hit a child.

Sara said, "Mark remembers all of it. And I'm sure you've noticed it left him with a slight stammer.

"Yes, but not always."

"I know. It's an emotional thing. Pops up now and then. He's been dealing with it for a long time. He's getting better."

Jess started to feel the burn and felt uncomfortable sitting on the couch. "Let's get some coffee."

They got up and went into the kitchen. Jess prepared coffee and put some cookies on a dish. They sat in the kitchen. Jess said, "Brenda has been very close-mouthed about Mark. She usually tells me everything. What's the story?"

"Mark isn't much better, but I can tell something's going on. I like her too.

"She's good for him."

"How did you meet Brenda?"

"We go way back. Grew up together in Massachusetts. But lost contact when we were at college. She married her high school sweetheart. He wasn't such a sweetheart."

Sara said, "I know what you mean."

"So she got rid of him and moved down here. I got a call from her and we picked up where we left off." Jess felt hot all over and a little sick to her stomach.

"Then you went into business together."

"Yup, that's how Event Services started."

They talked the rest of the evening until Jess started to yawn. "I'm sorry. Between all the salt air today and this damn sunburn, I'm knocked out."

"No wonder. You should go to sleep. Do you need anything before I leave?"

"No, I'm fine. And thanks for coming. I'll call you."

After Sara left, Jess climbed into bed. Before she fell asleep, she said, "Dear God, thank you for Sam."

CHAPTER 13

Sam and Frank drove up to the victim's house. Sam said, "It's a nice neighborhood. Quaint, but I like it." There were three steps leading up to a front porch. The body had been removed and the area cordoned off.

Frank said, "Shot the same way as Henry Dobson, in the back and before he could get to the front door."

"What does forensics say?"

Frank shrugged, "There's no exit wound. They'll be able to tell more about the gun when they get the bullet out."

"Did you notify the family?"

"Yeah. There's only the wife and she's so hysterical, we had to call a doctor to calm her down. But I think we lucked out. There's sort of an eyewitness."

"Let's go in and try to talk to her."

Sam liked the porch in front. Homey, but it needed a rocking chair. He remembered his folks sitting on the front porch during the summer. Most of the neighbors did. They caught up on most of the news around town that way. The house, a two-story, had a large dining room on the right and a living room on the left. Enough space for lots of company. On one side of the living room, pictures were displayed on a piano. Many were of a young man in a football uniform. A house full of love.

Hunched up on the couch, with tear stains on her face and a cup in her hand, Virginia Watson looked worn out. Sam asked the woman with her. "How is she?"

"Better now. I just made her a cup of tea."

Mrs. Watson said, "I hear you. What do you want?"

"My name is Sam Wesley and this is my partner, Frank Romano. We're going to find out who did this to your husband. Are you up to answering some questions?"

"Yes, I think so."

"Do you know of anyone who would want to hurt Mr. Watson?"

She started to cry and held her temples. "No. I don't understand it. He doesn't have an enemy in the world."

Sam continued to ask her the usual questions and with each answer, she became more upset. He didn't think she knew anything to help him.

"And you are...?" Sam asked the other woman.

She seemed a lot younger than Mrs. Watson.

"I'm Lori Landis. My family lives across the street. I took my dog out and while I stood in front of my house waiting, I saw someone run to the side of Virginia's house and he ducked into the yard. Most of our backyards adjoin. Then, I saw Bert lying on the porch. So I called the police."

"Can you describe the person you saw?"

"It was dark, but I think he was black and wore a baseball cap." She thought for a minute. "He may have been wearing glasses, but I'm not sure. He moved so fast."

"Mrs. Watson, is there anyone else in your family?"

She started to sob and answered, "My 16-year-old son, Tim."

She broke down again. "He's in the hospital. He got hurt playing football. Hit in the head and collapsed. They rushed him to the hospital. Now he's on life support with a brain injury. The doctors don't have much hope he'll recover."

Sam paused a few moments and walked over to the pictures on the piano and looked at them.

"I know you're going through a very difficult time. But I want to catch this killer and I know you do too. I'll try not to bother you too much longer."

"That's okay."

"How did your husband and son get along?"

"They were best buddies. Bert adored him, and I know Tim felt the same. Why do you ask?"

"It's just a routine question."

Mrs. Watson folded her arms and started to move her upper body back and forth holding herself together.

"Where did your husband go last night?"

"He started to see a psychiatrist a couple of nights a week. He thought Tim got hurt because of him."

"Why?"

"Well, Tim had a concussion about a month ago, and we thought he recovered. The doctor said he could go back to playing football but Tim didn't want to play anymore."

"So did he?"

"Yes, Bert told him not to be afraid and talked him into it. If he even suspected there'd be a problem, he never would have encouraged him."

"I need to have the name of your son's doctor. And could you give me the name and phone number of your husband's psychiatrist?"

"I think I have their cards. I'll get them for you."

When she left the room, Sam turned to the neighbor and asked, "As far as you know, would you agree with what Mrs. Watson said about her husband?"

"Yes, I would."

"Here they are." Mrs. Watson handed the cards to Sam.

"Thanks very much. I'll be in touch with you."

Outside, Sam turned to Frank, "The description of the person she saw, and the first one we got are the same."

"Yeah. Same person killed both of 'em."

"And I don't think he had a car. So, Frank, question some of the other neighbors. I'll check the backyard to see what I find."

Sam walked out back, going between the houses the neighbor mentioned. Mr. Watson must have chopped down one of the trees. It was lying in the yard. He probably didn't have time to tow it away. Sam walked right through the back neighbor's yard onto an adjoining street. The shooter must have run through and got away.

On the way home, he drove by an orange grove and breathed in the sweet smell. It helped ease the bad feeling he had. The poor guy. He loved his son and had a good life. Turned sour pretty quick. Sam reviewed his interviews. The descriptions of the stranger at both murder scenes were the same. Both victims were shot in the back. Mrs. Watson was genuinely distressed. No sign of parental abuse there. The only connections between the two cases he could make were they both had sons who incurred some kind of injury. He should talk to Mrs. Dobson again. Maybe both victims knew each other.

When Sam got home, he decided not to call Jess. He'd let her sleep. With a smile and a light heart, he continued to think about their day at the beach. She loved him. How about that? Not a complete surprise, but he wanted to know for sure. He could see spending the rest of his life with her, but he needed to tread with care. Show her she could trust him.

He hadn't eaten dinner, so he made a cheese omelet. He tried to swallow it while he thought about poor Mrs. Watson.

The next morning, Sam remembered his dream. Jess chopping down a tree, completely covered in calamine and dressed only in panties. The people in the neighborhood gathered around applauding. She bowed and said, "Now that I finished, I'm going to the beach and swim off some of this lotion." He couldn't remember the rest of it.

When Sam called Jess, she asked, "Is this who I think it is?"

"How's your sunburn?"

"I'm better. I think the vinegar scared it away. It almost scared Sara away."

"Oh good. She came over. How is she?"

"She's fine."

"I have a lot to do today, but I'll be finished by dinner time."

Jess pulled her legs over the side of the bed and examined them. "Oh, I'm not going anywhere. I've already called Brenda to let her know I can't come in. I'll go back to work tomorrow."

"Then, I'll bring dinner."

"Will it be gourmet?"

"I'll see what I can come up with."

"Do you know why I love you?"

"I know, 'cause I can cook."

"I'm thinking other things, but cooking's good too."

Sam laughed. "See you later."

CHAPTER 14

Jerry Dobson answered the door. "Hi, Mr. Wesley. C'mon in.

Jerry was more animated than the last time he spoke to Sam. He was flipping the wrist of his good hand playing with a yoyo.

"Hi, Jerry. Is your mother here?"

"No, she went to the store. We're out of milk again."

"Is it all right if I wait?"

"Sure."

"How's your arm."

"Much better thanks."

Jerry was comfortable with Sam today. "I see you're in the middle of a Monopoly game. Who's winning?"

"Just when I got a good winning streak goin', she decided to go the store. She always does that."

"I could take her place for a while. Mind if I play?"

Jerry's eyes were bright and for the first time,

Sam saw him smile. "Cool!"

Sam shook the dice and said "Say, Jerry. Could you do me a favor and think back to when you played Monopoly the night your father died?"

"Okay."

"Did your mother go to the store then?"

"Yeah. She did."

Jerry concentrated while he moved his piece around the board. They both looked up when they heard a key in the door.

"Hi, Mr. Wesley, another visit?"

"Yes. I wanted to let you know your husband's case is still open."

"Did you find anything out?"

"No, but there's been another homicide, and the circumstances are much like your husband's. I'm thinking there may be a connection there. Take your time and think back. Have you ever met anyone by the name of Bert Watson?"

"No. I don't think so. Jerry, go and watch TV please."

"Do I have to?"

"Yes, now go."

Jerry sulked and walked out of the room.

Sam said, "I still need to see your gun, Mrs. Dobson. You don't have an alibi, so we need to rule out your involvement in the shooting. It would be a lot easier if you turned it over to me now."

Mrs. Dobson was angry. "What do you mean—I don't have an alibi?"

"Jerry told me you went to the store the night Mr. Dobson died. How long were you at the store?"

"Not long at all. Let me call my attorney to see if it's okay to give you the gun."

"Fine."

She made her call and returned with the gun. "My lawyer says it's okay. And it's not my gun, it's my husband's. I've got nothing to hide. Will you leave us alone now?"

"If everything checks out and nothing else comes up, I'll try not to bother you again."

He put the gun in a plastic bag and left. Took out his cell. "Frank, I got the gun."

"No kiddin', how come?"

"Her lawyer said OK—and I got it."

"Great. What next."

"I'm on my way there so you can get it to ballistics. I'm gonna go talk to Tim Watson's doctor and also the psychiatrist his father saw."

"By the way, Sam, the bullet they found in Watson. It's the same caliber as Dobson's."

"Well, another connection. They should be able to find out if it came from the same gun. So tell forensics to hurry it up."

Sam went to Memorial Hospital next to see Tim Watson's doctor, and when he came down to meet him Sam asked, "Has there been any change in Tim's condition?"

"I'm afraid not. As I told his parents, I'm not at all sure he'll recover."

"Doctor, I understand he sustained a concussion a month or so before this last injury. Could it have been as a result of a beating?"

"Not at all. I know it happened on the football field."

"Okay, thanks for your time. I appreciate it."

Sam visited Mr. Watson's psychiatrist who confirmed what Mrs. Watson already told him—he felt guilty because he'd encouraged his son to continue to play football.

**

On his way home, Sam started to plan dinner. He decided on a Caesar salad, chicken l'orange, rice and asparagus. The chicken was made and in the freezer, and he stopped at his favorite market to buy the romaine lettuce, asparagus and hard-crusted rolls. He walked along the crowded aisles and found the best lettuce and asparagus and the crispiest rolls. At his apartment, he defrosted the main dish, made the salad and steamed the asparagus.

If she didn't already love me, this meal would seal the deal. Hey, another slogan—"Seal the Deal Meal."

On his way to Jess's, he could smell the delicious food he packed up and felt less frustrated about his two unsolved case. He was sure they were connected, but how?

Jess looked much better. She didn't have as much calamine on and he could tell she fussed with her hair. She wore a pair of shorts and a sleeveless top.

Her appetite returned but their meal was interrupted when the phone rang.

Jess said, "Damn, who's that?" then picked up. "Hello."

"Hey Jessica. It's Mmark Janus. My mother hurt her ffoot. She carried a bunch of ppackages and fell over one of those parking space barriers. She's in a lot of pain and I don't know what to do!"

"Take it easy Mark. Sam's here and we'll be right over."

"Thanks Jess and hurry!"

When they got to Mark's, he was a wreck. Sara said, "Hi you two. My son overreacted as usual. I'm not in much pain, but he gets so upset when the smallest thing is wrong with me."

Mark interrupted her. "It's not small. I saw you llimp a little and your fface showed a lot of pain."

"Let's take a look." Sam bent down and raised her leg. Sara could move her swollen ankle around with no pain.

Mark said, "I'll be right back."

Sara said, "He's too nervous to watch. He's probably gone to wash his hands."

"If my first aid experience is correct, I don't think it's serious." Sam said. "Just apply ice for 15 minutes and then apply heat. If it's not better tomorrow, you should have it x-rayed."

Mark returned and said, "Let's go to the hospital nnow. Why wait until ttomorrow?" He became more agitated and started to speak louder.

"Mark, stop it." Sara scolded. "You're making a big thing out of nothing. Let's do what Sam says."

"But Mom, I really ththink we should go now."

"I mean it, Mark. Stop it. You called Jess and ruined their dinner without thinking. I told you not to. Get hold of yourself. This is nothing."

"It's not nothing. What if it's bbroken?"

"It's not broken. I can move it. Enough."

"Okay, bbut I don't agree."

***

When they returned to their cold meal, Sam said, "He sure gets worked up a lot."

"I know. He doesn't seem to be able to handle anything the least bit unpleasant. Strange, when he had a recent plumbing emergency, he reacted in much the same way. I guess it's the result of a bad childhood. Otherwise, he's a pretty nice guy, don't you think?"

"He is. But I bet he won't sleep much tonight worrying. Worriers don't sleep well."

Jess resumed eating and made a face. "The crisis is over, so let's finish this wonderful meal, but could you warm it up first?"

"I live to be your slave, madam." Sam teased.

"Keep that in mind later on."

CHAPTER 15

Jess sat down at her desk and was careful not to rub her sunburned legs against the chair. Brenda asked, "What's with you?"

"The remains of a killer sunburn. I'm much better now after Sam's home remedy."

Brenda, with a thoughtful expression, rubbed her chin. "Oh, is that good for sunburns too?"

"Get your mind out of the gutter, Bren. It's really his mother's special remedy. The application of vinegar. Gets the heat out of the burn."

"Ugh. The thought makes me want to stay in the dark forever."

Jess fired up her computer. "It wasn't bad. Anyway, here I am. What's new?"

Brenda walked over to Jess and dropped a clipboard on her desk."

"Things are under control. Business is slowing down a little, so I see Mark more often."

"Really?"

"Yes, and guess what? I went to a church service with him last week."

"Sounds as though he's serious."

"Maybe. But he's afraid to commit. We drove by the little church around the corner, and I heard about the inspiring priest there, so I suggested we go in.

"Did it help?"

"I think so. Father Simpson delivered a terrific sermon and we enjoyed it. In fact, it impressed Mark so much he wants his mother to attend one of the services there."

Jess frowned. "What's his first name?"

"I think it's Alan."

"I've heard the name before. I saw something about a Rev. Alan Simpson in the paper. Used to be at a church on the East Coast. Maybe it's not the same one, because that Rev. Simpson molested a few altar boys. He said he didn't do it and they couldn't prove he did. It might be the same guy."

Brenda waved her off and shook her head. "Oh Jess, I don't think so. It couldn't be the same person. Anyway, after church, we went out for lunch, and Mark asked me not to date anyone else."

"That's great, Bren. I knew you'd hit it off."

"It's more than hitting it off."

"Do you love him?"

"Jess, I find myself thinking about him and smiling all the time. He's the best thing that has happened to me since I've been in Florida. I do love him."

They got down to business and Jess tried to concentrate, but the backs of her thighs were uncomfortable. She tried to sit with her legs elevated, but they still hurt. Then she stood while she worked. Not good either. She gave up. "Brenda, I think I have to go home and lie down with my legs in the air."

Brenda forced another concerned look. "Okay, you certainly know how to do that, and I'm sure you always feel better afterward."

Jess went into gales of laughter, "All right Brenda, I guess I asked for it. See you tomorrow."

***

After she got home, she changed into her sunburn outfit—shorts and a halter. Called Sam as she went into the kitchen and started to fill the coffee pot. "Hi, are you busy?"

"To whom am I speaking?"

"Whom do you think?"

"Sunburn Sally?"

"Bingo."

"What's up?"

"I decided to come home early and change into something comfortable. My legs are a problem."

"They're no problem for me."

"I'm not kidding. Anyway, I'm home if you have time to come by."

"I wish I could honey, but I'm tied up here with paperwork. I just found out my only suspect's gun wasn't used for either of the two murders. So, we're back to the drawing board. Believe me, I'd much rather be with you."

She tried not to sound disappointed. "Okay, I should waddle down to see Sara anyway. Her ankle is much better, but she still has it elevated. Maybe I can help her."

"Give her my best, and you take it easy. I'll talk to you tomorrow. I love you, Sally."

"I love you too, wise guy."

***

Jess knocked on Sara's door. She answered with slippers on and an Ace bandage on her ankle. "I didn't want you to get up, so I tried the door but couldn't get in."

"I always lock the door. It's a habit I formed when we lived in Chicago. This is the first floor, so I'm more comfortable when I know it's locked."

"How's your ankle?"

"It's better. I can walk without a limp now. How's your sunburn?"

Jess sat on the edge of the sofa. "It's better too, but I had to leave work early. I still can't rub my thighs on anything. Can I do something for you?"

"No. I'm fine, but I can use the company."

Jess bent over and took a candy from the dish on the coffee table. "Good. Say, did you ever speak to Richard about your going to visit his son?"

"Yes, and I took your advice and told him I'd go with him but not right now."

The caramel, a little old and sticky, made it hard for Jess to open her mouth and talk, "What did he say?"

"He said he understood why I wanted to wait. Then the poor man started to tell me the ordeal he faces every time he visits."

"What ordeal?"

"Richard said every time he sees the boy, he feels cheated because he's not normal. He can't understand why parents take their children for granted and sometimes even hurt them."

Jess thought that sounded weird. "He probably shouldn't focus on the boy so much. Try to enjoy life more."

"I felt so sorry for him. I didn't know what to say, so I just listened."

Jess accidentally moved her leg against the sofa and moaned. "He's such a nice guy. It must be hard to accept. I'm sure seeing you helps."

"I hope so. We've had some wonderful times together. It's been good for me too."

"About wonderful times, I understand Brenda and Mark see each other often and they went to church together."

"They did and Mark asked if I wanted to come the next time they go."

"Will you?"

"I think so. I may ask Richard to come along. He might find some comfort there."

CHAPTER 16

Sam slurped his coffee while he and Frank brainstormed. "I think we hit a wall. Any ideas?"

Frank tapped a pencil on his open notebook. "Let's see. The description of the person at both scenes is the same. Since the parking attendant didn't see him leave the night of Dobson's murder, we can assume the killer had been waiting for him."

Sam played with the swinging pendulum on his desk. "He must have been tracking Dobson because he knew his car would be parked in the garage. The same with the Watson murder. The killer followed Watson home. He must have known about his psychiatrist's appointment."

Frank stood and threw up his hands. "It's a piece of cake, Sam. All we need to do is find a thin, black man who wears glasses and a baseball cap. How many people with that description do you think there are in this city?"

Sam wondered if he missed an obvious clue.

"Yeah right. But the one important fact we do have is the same person killed both victims."

"We also know the killer walked both times. The first time, the parking attendant didn't see him come back down with his car, and the second, a neighbor saw the killer run away."

"And the neighbors didn't see any strange cars."

"Okay Sam, he's a walker. So, probably he doesn't live too far from his victims. What else?"

Sam started to enumerate, "Both victims were fathers of injured sons. The same gun killed both of them and they were shot in the back. Their sons were treated at Memorial Hospital." He paused. "Damn! Maybe that's a fact we can explore. What do you think?"

"A hell of a coincidence no doubt. It's a busy hospital, but it could be how the killer found his victims. We need to find a motive, Sam."

Sam stood and pushed his chair in. "Yuh, we need to go to Memorial and find out what the process is when a new patient is seen. I'll go. You re-interview the families, maybe we overlooked something there."

***

With the help of the hospital administrator, Sam compiled a list of most of the people involved in the initial interviewing of patients. They might learn more by doing background checks on all of them. He met Frank and gave him the list to do the checks.

Frank told him he got nothing more from the two victims' wives, and Dobson's girlfriend had a credible alibi.

Sam stretched. "We'll pick it up tomorrow."

***

Driving home, Sam's thoughts turned to Jess. "The last few months were wonderful. Would it be too soon to ask her? He stopped by a jewelry store.

He talked to the salesman at length about rings, the weight of the diamonds, their color and cost. There were so many to choose from but he saw the one he wanted. It would look beautiful on her finger. Said he'd be back soon.

Afraid he'd tell her about the ring, Sam resisted calling Jess. He wasn't ready to say anything yet. Instead, he decided to celebrate his decision by making himself a noodle kugel. He had all the ingredients and it would keep his mind occupied. He started filling up a large pot of water, salted it and put it on the stove to boil. He combined the eggs, cottage cheese, sour cream, sugar, salt, a spritz of lemon and his special ingredient, crushed pineapple.

When should he ask her? He'll know when the time is right. Maybe he should buy the ring now to be ready.

He added the noodles and when they were al dente and drained, he added some butter and the rest of his prepared ingredients, poured it all into a casserole dish, sprinkled it with breadcrumbs, dotted it with butter and put it into the oven. His mouth watered. *Tomorrow I'm goin' on a diet.*

The next morning, Jess called. "Hi, I missed you last night."

"How's the sunburn?"

"All better. I just got to work. Decided to make an early start after goofing off yesterday. Brenda says hello."

"Hello back."

She wants us to come to a birthday party she's having for Mark next Sunday night. Will you come?"

"Let me see what my schedule says for next weekend. Friday, Jess; Saturday, Jess; Sunday, Jess. No, I'm busy. Who is this?"

"You're an idiot. Will I see you tonight, too."

"If I have to. I'll call you later. I love you, Jessica."

"Me too."

CHAPTER 17

*T*he Avenger sits at a bare table with the newspaper opened, turning pages at a feverish pace, reading the positive report of society to avoid injustices of the world. Attempting to pacify the pain in the brain, The Avenger's eyes rest on a news report which appears on the very last page under "Community News." It's entitled "Child Molester Leads 'Gays' in Scout Protest." It goes on to say that Donald Trent was wrongly convicted as a child molester and was released. Mr. Trent has always been an exemplary Boy Scout leader with many awards and resents the label of Child Molester which is completely untrue. He says he is an example of the type of person who should be a Boy Scout leader and that being gay has nothing to do with the fact that he is a great scoutmaster.

After reading the article, The Avenger walks to the sink and after a full hand scrub sits at the table. The Voice intensifies and a creative plan emerges.

Under the stabbing gush of the shower, The Avenger con-

fers with The Voice. Then focuses on what must be done.

***

Outside the school, where the Boy Scout meeting is held, The Avenger waits. They should be out soon. Ah! There they are. The young boys crowding around one of the leaders enrages The Avenger. The leader breaks away from his flock and The Avenger picks up the leader's trail at the next corner—just far enough not to be noticed.

***

Donald Trent, a Boy Scout leader, loved the meetings, camping trips and enjoyed mentoring the young scouts. Way back at an early age, he had always been the brunt of bullying because he was gay. Being interested in the Boy Scouts gave him the leadership skills that helped his self-esteem. He would never abuse the privilege of showing other young people how to be a valuable person in society.

Donald arrived at his house and opened the mailbox. His back exploded, and he fell face down on the flagstone walk.

CHAPTER 18

For the past week, both detectives were busy following up on the Memorial Hospital employee backgrounds. It took a lot of time with no results. They were frustrated. Frank didn't learn anything more from either of the two widows when he went back to talk to them.

At a coffee break, Sam eyed the doughnut box on Frank's desk. "I told you I'm on a diet, why in hell did you have to buy those things?"

"I'm not on a diet."

Sam thought about tasting a honey-dipped doughnut. "Well, you damn well should be."

"I need the sugar rush to get my mind going."

"Your mind already went."

"Be serious, Sam. We're gettin' nowhere." I hope these cases don't get cold."

"Just take one step at a time. Something will turn up. It always does. Just when you think you've thought of everything, a light bulb goes on."

"Yeah, right."

Sam pulled himself out of the chair and glanced at the doughnuts one more time. "Keep thinking. I have to go. Got an important errand. See you Monday."

***

He went back to the jewelry store. Sam wanted to take this step for his and Jess's future ever since he saw the ring. When the salesman showed it to him again, Sam took out his checkbook. "That's it. Tell me how much."

He felt great. Even after spending so much money. The velvet box in his jacket pocket reassured him this was the right thing to do.

When should I give it to her? Not this weekend, she'll be busy working and then we're going to Mark's birthday party. I want it to be perfect and in a romantic setting.

After he got home Sam hid the box in a safe place and checked his food supplies. He needed stuff for the following week, made a list and went to his favorite market.

He walked up an aisle crowded with fruits and vegetables and tried not to buy too much. He raised each piece of fruit and smelled it before putting it into the bag. Made sure all the veggies were crisp. Prices were higher here but worth it.

He almost bought ingredients to prepare an engagement dinner but changed his mind. I'll be too nervous to cook. I'll take her someplace special.

He bought what he needed and joined a line to pay. Everyone in the store knew Sam and kidded around with him. Jess would like this place. Next time, I'll take her.

When Sunday came around, he called Jess, "How about I pick you up and we go for a long walk?"

"You're kidding. I've been on my feet for three days straight. I'd rather take a nap."

"Okay, may I join you?"

"Yes, you may."

"I'll be right over."

He almost took the ring with him but changed his mind. He needed to do it right. He'd wait.

Sam got there and joined Jess in bed where they stayed until Sam left to dress for Mark's party.

***

Brenda decorated her whole house in honor of Mark's birthday and even created an enormous sign at the entrance. Sam and Jess joined Mark, Sara and Richard who were having drinks on the lanai. Brenda looked radiant and Mark couldn't take his eyes off her. Even though the group hadn't been together for a while, the conversation continued where they had left off. Brenda told everyone to bring joke gifts, and Mark chuckled after he opened each one. Then Brenda presented him with a beautiful watch. "This is fantastic." He took her in his arms and kissed her—ignoring all the teasing.

Jess didn't hear a hint of a stammer, and she saw how right they were for each other. Brenda helped him be himself.

At dinner, Sam said, "Brenda, everything is so good. No diet tonight. You're a great cook."

Not really. I called our caterer and wallah! It's magic. Ready-made cuisine."

Jess said, "You're too honest, Bren. They never would have guessed."

"So what? It gave me more time to clean and decorate, and as Father Simpson says, 'We must be honest and true to ourselves.'"

"Did you go to church this morning?"

Sara chimed in. "All four of us went and the priest's sermon motivated us to look within ourselves for answers."

Richard agreed. "He helped me to think about my situation in a different way."

Mark said, "Yes, inspiring. But I must say for me—tarnished."

Jess asked, "Why?"

"Brenda told me you thought he may be the priest who abused children on the East Coast. I looked him up on the internet and I think he's the same person. Although, I must admit it's a little hard to believe. He seems so genuine. If he did do those terrible things, he's a master at hiding his true character."

Brenda commented, "Oh, Mark. Don't get so serious!"

"It's a serious thing, but I'll be glad to change the subject. Sam, can you tell us more about those murder cases you were working on?"

"I wish I could. We're not much closer to catching the killer than before. We have a description and a few connections."

"What's his description?"

"It may not be accurate. I couldn't tell you anyway."

"Can you tell us what the connections are between the victims?"

"I guess so, but they're probably coincidental. Both had injured sons treated at Memorial Hospital."

"And what else."

"That's about it."

Jess decided to lighten the conversation. "Sam, tell them about the nuisance cases you get."

Sam proceeded to repeat the amusing stories he told Jess when they were at the beach. He continued, "Another favorite of mine is when we were called because of a disturbance at a local sports bar and restaurant. A woman got stuck inside a toilet bowl for 20 minutes after the seat broke. The handicapped toilet seat she sat on cracked and dumped her into the bowl."

They held their sides laughing. Brenda, barely able to ask, "What did you do?"

"We got her out and just wrote up the report, but she sued the toilet seat manufacturer."

Mark asked, "Did she get hurt?"

"She claimed injury to her hip. But who knows."

Richard piped up. "Truth is stranger than fiction. You couldn't make this stuff up."

Brenda said, "It's still early. Let's play a game of charades. Are you up for it, Sam?"

"After three glasses of wine, I'm up for anything."

They formed two teams. Because there were six of them, Jess and Sam split up. Both teams fooled around and took a long time guessing except for Sam and Jess. It turned out to be a match between them. Whenever it was their turn, their respective teammates cheered them on. Sam was surprised Jess pantomimed so expertly. Sam couldn't beat her time.

They continued to joke around until they said their goodbyes.

***

Reliving the evening on their way home, Jess said, "So, you couldn't beat the champion charade player, huh?"

"Not tonight. I was under the influence of wine. There will be a rematch, and I will win. But tonight, I'm ready to show you what I do best."

Jess said, "We'll see about that. Sam, you know Mark opened up this evening and he didn't stammer once. But his interest in your cases surprised me."

"Yeah. Sorry I couldn't tell him more."

"Can you tell me what description you got of the killer?"

"Okay but mind you, it's a hypothetical description."

"Right."

"He's a thin black man who wears a baseball cap and thick glasses. Not very distinctive. Witnesses in each of the two murders gave us the same description."

"That's something anyway."

Jess leaned back on the seat and sighed. "Nice evening, wasn't it? They loved hearing your silly stories. If possible, I love you even more tonight."

Sam reached over and pulled her close to him. "I can't wait to get you home, so you can tell me more."

Now would be a good time to propose but I don't have the damn ring.

Sam's cell rang. "What is it, Frank?"

"Another shooting. This time a Boy Scout leader. You better come down here. It's not far from Jess's house."

After Sam got the address he gave Jess a quick kiss, dropped her off at her building and drove off.

CHAPTER 19

Sam arrived minutes later. Frank, the medical examiner and several other forensic people were there. Police held the onlookers back. Sam said to the examiner, "Talk to me."

"Shot in the back and the bullet went right through. We found it."

After the body was carried away and the scene cleared, Sam asked, "What do you know about him?"

"His name is Donald Trent. He lives here with another man. I think they're a couple. Anyway, this guy doesn't have any idea who'd want to kill Donald. His parents live in Tallahassee and they're being notified."

Sam breathed a very long sigh, "Starting to look like it's a serial killer, Frank. "It's too late now, but tomorrow let's check the neighbors' stories and do a thorough background check on Mr. Trent. We'll see if that gives us anything."

When Sam had trouble sleeping that night, he tried to think only of Jess. That helped him relax and get a decent night's rest.

***

When Sam got to the station the next day, he found Frank typing. "My, my how efficient. Back to work already!"

"Just updating my notes on the backgrounds of most of the Memorial Hospital people. I'm done for now. Still have a pile of names to go through."

After Frank pulled the paper out of the dated typewriter, he handed the list to Sam. "Let's see." His eyes skimmed the report and he put it in his top drawer.

"Now, about our new murder. Frank, call Donald's folks and see what you can find out about him. Also, check Tallahassee's crime records and see if he pops up. I'll go back to the neighborhood and ask around."

Sam limped back to his car. The damn leg again. Maybe he should have asked Frank to walk that neighborhood. Eh! He'd better stop whining, suck it up and be a man. He tried to put more weight on the leg so he wouldn't limp as much. Felt lucky compared to the poor dead guy.

Jess lived nearby, so Sam was familiar with the neighborhood. Nothing turned up on the house-to-house. No one knew anything about Donald Trent. They did see him and the roomie together a lot. Sam figured he probably was gay, but that's no

112

crime.

After canvassing, Sam stopped by Jess's and hoped she'd be home. She greeted him in her morning attire—sweat suit and bare feet—looking a little pale without her makeup. "How about a cup of coffee?"

"Hey. What a nice surprise. Just had one myself." They kissed and walked into the kitchen. "What's up?"

Sam poured himself a cup, put his arm around Jess's shoulders. "Another one of those 'shot-in-the-back' murders. Between us, I think we're dealing with a serial killer—hypothetically of course."

Jess's interest was aroused. "Why do you think so?"

"Well, for one thing three murders happened in the same vicinity within a very short period of time. That in itself is unusual. Another thing, the M.O. is the same as the others."

"So you think the same person did all three?"

"I think so, but it's more of a gut feeling."

"I'm getting creeped out. Maybe I should go to one of those Florida gun shops and get me a pistol."

"It's not funny, Jess. I want you to be careful. Don't go around walking in the dark by yourself."

"Okay, my big strong man. Say, I took today off to clean, but how about we spend time together instead."

"Oh Jess! It's a tempting—a very tempting offer,

but I've got to get back to work." He got up ready to go.

"Are you sure? I promise you a good time."

"Oh Honey, you're killing me! I can't, I really can't. I've gotta go."

She kissed him several times until he forcibly pulled himself away, "Talk to you later, and you're a tease."

She smiled. "So long, sweet cheeks."

He shook his head and went out the door.

Jess resumed her vacuuming and suddenly felt queasy. She dashed to the bathroom and threw up last night's meal. She ate and drank too much. Served her right. Never again. She splashed her face with cold water and felt a lot better.

She continued to clean. Too bad Sam couldn't stay. It would have been a hell of a lot better than vacuuming and dusting.

Again, she felt a wave of nausea and stopped cleaning. She felt a little dizzy. She sat and thought back.

It couldn't be. We were careful, weren't we? There was that one time. But I haven't missed my period—although the last one was very brief. It's not fair. We've been so happy. I never thought I'd have a child. If I'm pregnant, it might change everything. Before I get ahead of myself, I better find out now.

She showered, dressed and walked to the drug-store. There were so damn many home pregnancy tests. It took a while to decide. Brought it home, followed the directions and sat on the side of the bathtub to wait for the results. Kind of numb, Jess couldn't pinpoint what her reaction would be. Hurry up! It's taking forever.

What if? Should she tell him? She didn't want him to feel pressured to marry her. She loved him, but did she even want to get married again? Why was she still afraid? Sam wasn't like her jerk ex-husband.

Better see the color of the stick before she gets more nervous.

She looked. "Ohhhh, I'm sooo happy!"

CHAPTER 20

Grimacing at the shooting pain in his leg, Sam flopped into his chair. "Tell me about Donald Trent. I got nothing from the neighbors."

Frank started to read his notes. "Trent had an interesting situation in Tallahassee. Accused of raping a 10-year-old boy in his troop when he was an assistant Boy Scout leader. Case was dismissed because Trent's part in it was unclear. Shortly afterward, the little kid committed suicide."

Sam started to feel less sad about Donald Trent. The poor parents of that child. Sending him to Boy Scout camp to learn how to be an honorable person. Then something like this happened. He felt less enthusiastic about catching his killer.

"So it could be that maybe the same thing happened here. Interview the kids in the troop. Ask each parent to be present when the child is questioned."

"Okay. I'll get on it. Who do you think could have killed him?"

"I don't know, but it could be an upset parent of one of the boys in his troop here, or it could be a parent of the boy who killed himself. Maybe we should get in touch with Tallahassee and get their address and phone number. I can do that. I want to talk to them."

They were busy for the rest of the afternoon setting up appointments for the next day. Frank to interview the boys in Trent's troop and Sam would drive to Tallahassee.

"Frank, I'd like to run something by you."

"What."

"Trent was shot with the same gun that killed the other victims and found in the same position as the other victims. So, in that way this case is similar. But in the other two cases, the victims were fathers of children who were abused or not treated as they should have been. So, what's different here and what's the same here?"

After a pause, Frank answered, "The same situation is that children were being abused by the shooting victim, and the victims lived near each other. The difference is that in this case, it wasn't the father."

"That's right. How did the killer know about the past history of this guy? Could he be a parent of one of the troop children? If so, the parent killed the abuser rather than being the abuser."

Frank came back, "Maybe the murderer isn't either but he read about it somewhere and wanted to be a Good Samaritan."

"It's a stretch but possible. We'll find out if our local paper reported anything about it. I'm going to call them."

Sam called the Herald. After he introduced himself and explained what he wanted, the man asked him to hold. After a while Sam got his answer. "Sure enough. There was a story about Trent coming here after being cleared of a rape in Tallahassee. Stuck on the back page, so a person would have had to read that paper from cover to cover to see it." Sam thanked him and asked that they send him a copy.

Sam turned to Frank, "You may be right about the Good Samaritan theory."

***

During the boring ride to Tallahassee, Sam wished that Jess could've kept him company. But after all, she does have a business and a career. He shouldn't be so selfish.

Still trying to find just the right time to propose, he regretted missing the first opportunity. Maybe he should carry the ring around all the time. Nah, it would be just his luck that he'd lose it. Excited to imagine her reaction, he wanted to savor that thought for a while. The time will come. He knew it.

He had a hard time finding the address of the boy's parents but called them and they talked him to their house. They were nice people, and Sam found it hard to find the right words to ask about their boy.

"When did you find out what was happening?"

"Not until my boy finally unburdened himself and told us about it. I would say about a month after he joined the Scouts. He said that one of the leaders kept approaching him and put him in situations where they were alone. Jimmy tried to discourage him but when the troop went on a camping trip, it happened."

Jimmy's mother started to cry, "When he came home, he couldn't talk about it to me. He told his father and then we pulled him out of the Scouts. The whole thing was too much for Jimmy and he ended it."

Sam felt so bad for them, he couldn't continue the interview. Nothing else needed to be cleared up.

"Thank you very much for seeing me. I'm so sorry it turned out that way for Jimmy."

Sam drove home and tried to think about what he would cook for his dinner and for the first time, he couldn't switch his mind off the rotten side of humanity. That bastard, another guy who deserved to die. If Sam were lucky enough to ever have a child, he'd be honored to love and to care for him. And that would apply to any kid entrusted to his care.

He then decided to think about Jess again. That worked better. He remembered their fun day at the beach and wanted to go back soon.

CHAPTER 21

After putting in a full work day, Jess dragged herself home and sat in a hot bath. She lay back feeling the hot water and moist air all around her. The day seemed to float away. She started to doze off but shook herself awake. She needed to take a step back and assess the situation and Sam as a father. He's a cop and in danger a lot. That wouldn't be good, would it? But he loves his job and is smart and careful.

Should she keep the baby? What am I saying, of course I'll keep my baby. That's not the question. Should we get married just because we're having a baby? Huh, Sam wouldn't have it any other way.

Do I want to get married again? Will he turn out to be unfaithful too?

Who am I kidding. It would be wonderful to be married to Sam; thoughtful, gentle and loyal and he'd be a fantastic father. I'll have to think about it some more. Don't want to pressure him. I think I need a second opinion and know just the person to call.

She dried off and called Sara. "Hi, I need someone to talk to. Can you come up?"

"I'm just sitting and vegetating in front of the TV. I'd love to see you. Be right there."

Sara came in carrying a banana bread. "Just took this out of the oven. If you brew some coffee, we can have a piece now."

"It smells wonderful. Let's go to the kitchen."

While they were snacking, Sara said, "It's all right to eat banana bread because it has fruit in it and it's nourishing. Probably it's not even fattening."

"Yeah, right, if you say so."

"So, tell me honey, what's on your mind."

With a big sigh, "I don't know. I'm confused about Sam."

"What do you mean?"

"Don't get me wrong, I'm very much in love with him and he is with me, but it's where we go from here that puzzles me. I'm gunshy because of my failed marriage, and I'm not sure how Sam feels about the next step. I don't want to screw things up and ask him. I'm not sure myself."

"How can I help?"

Jess tried to get her thoughts together so they wouldn't sound muddled and confusing.

"Sara, I know very little about your marriage, and I wonder what happened to make it go sour. Would it be too painful for you to share that with me?"

"No. It might be good to talk about it. When I married David, we were very much in love and very happy. He worshipped me, and I adored him. He was a successful architect and often entertained clients with drinks and dinner.

"Sounds like a good life."

"Yes, but the drinking became a problem. He tried stopping but couldn't. His work suffered and they let him go. He decided to start his own business but the drinking just got worse and we had no money. He started to borrow money wherever he could get it."

"Is that when he started hitting Mark?"

"He never wanted children. Even before he started drinking, he resented the attention I gave to Mark from the time that he was a baby. It might sound weird, but he was jealous of our son and took all his frustrations out on him."

"Did you leave him?"

"We separated and I got a job. Mark became his old self again. He's always been my whole world, and I don't for a minute regret that I had him. Once I held that little bundle in my arms, I felt so blessed, and the joy of him increased as he got older."

"What about his father?"

"He's out of the picture. He got into a brawl and someone hit him in the head and he died. Jessica, my experience is not necessarily yours. I ignored the nagging feelings I had about him and married him anyway. That won't happen to you."

"How will I know?"

"Jess, I think you know already. I know you had a different marriage. You said he was unfaithful, is that right? I bet you wonder if Sam would be unfaithful too.

"Yes."

"Right now, do you have a gut feeling that he would be unfaithful?"

"No."

"And deep down, is there any doubt in your mind that he is completely unselfish?"

"No."

"I've always thought that when there is doubt about anything at all, listen to your body as well as your head. If you have a question in your mind you must listen to it. And honey, if there was a problem, you'd know it by now."

Tears started to fall down Jess's cheeks, "Oh Sara, I love you."

Sara embraced her, "I love you too."

After Sara left, Jess wondered why she didn't tell her about the baby. Maybe it was because once she said the words, she'd have to believe it, or maybe she just wanted to get used to the idea of becoming a mother.

Jess felt a whole lot better. Sara really helped, but she didn't think she'd tell Sam about the baby for a little while. She had to wait for the right time.

CHAPTER 22

Frank was reviewing his recent interviews with Sam. "I spoke to most of the kids in the troop. Nothing new. The boys liked Trent, and I couldn't find anything unusual there. A dead end, so to speak."

"You're right. It might be a good idea to get away from this for a while. Maybe get a new perspective. I'd like to take a few days off. Would you mind taking over?"

Frank flashed a smile. "No problem."

Sam wanted to be with Jess in the worst way. So he called. "Hi, my love, how about us going somewhere for a few days? I think we both need it. When can you get away?"

Jess checked her calendar, "Oh that would be wonderful. But I can't go over the weekend. I have bookings. So, will tomorrow be too soon?

"That's perfect. I'll call and make reservations. How about driving up to Savannah?"

"A great idea. Believe it or not, I've never been there. It's supposed to be a beautiful city. I'll start packing immediately."

"Okay. Don't go overboard with the clothes. You won't need a lot."

"Sam Wesley! I'm shocked."

"Good."

"Let me know what time I have to be ready."

"I'll call right away."

He reserved a room in one of the nicest hotels and rushed home to pack and bring his dog to the kennel. He and Jess agreed he should sleep over at her condo so they could start out early.

At first, when Sam thought about getting away, he toyed with the idea of proposing on this trip. But then decided he wanted to be on their home turf when he gave her the ring. It would make it more real.

On their way to Savannah, Jess opened her window and let the wind mess her hair. "Sam, why haven't you thought of doing this before, I feel so free, don't you."

"No, because you captured my heart."

"Cut the bullshit."

"Oh my. I thought you were a proper lady, I may have to reassess."

"I'm serious. A change of scenery is always good. Let's put on some music."

"No, I'd rather talk.

"Okay."

Jess tried to squelch her curiosity about Sam's marriage. She knew it was a sensitive subject for him, but she needed to hear about it. "Would it be too painful to tell me about Sondra and your marriage?"

"No, it hurt for a long time but the scars are healed over. Sondra and I knew each other as friends for a few years, then the situation changed and we fell in love. We were very happy for the first three years. We even started to talk about having a child. Then she found out she had breast cancer; a kick in the head for both of us, but we went through all the treatments. She was clear for a while, but it came back and she died. I felt guilty for a long time. I don't know why. They tell me that all survivors think that way."

"Oh Sam, that's so sad."

"Yup it is, but it's in the past. I have to move on, although I'll never forget Sondra and our life together. What about you? I mean your marriage, what happened?"

"I met Steve in college and we got married after graduation. He made most of our decisions. Probably my fault. But soon I realized he didn't want me to make any at all. When I said I wanted children, he said 'We have plenty of time for kids. Who wants to be tied down.'"

"That must've been hard for you to hear."

"Yeah. Then, he started coming home late a couple of times a week, making all sorts of excuses. I smelled another woman on him after he got into bed one night and that was it. I filed for divorce after that. You know, I feel guilty too. The death of a marriage. I kept thinking I did something to drive him away."

"Jessica, I can tell you from first-hand experience, you didn't. You are the most wonderful, loving woman I've ever known—and that's true. I love you so much it hurts, and I'll never disappoint you."

"Now you're making me cry."

"Well, hold those tears, we're here. Let's check in."

They loved the city and on the first day they walked and walked. Sam bought her a few trinkets and Jess bought him a sweater. He said he never wears sweaters. She bought it anyway, because it made him look sexy.

The second day, they spent in the room making love most of the time. Before they knew it, they had to pack up and leave.

Jess threw her clothes in the suitcase, "I never fold when I'm returning from a trip. Two days is a tease, I could spend a month here."

"I don't know if I'd have the energy."

On the way home, they took turns singing, then sang in harmony and then got so silly they couldn't sing at all. "Who has the worst voice?" Sam asked.

Jess wiped her eyes, "It's a toss-up. Let's give it a rest, I can't laugh anymore, my side hurts."

They calmed down, and it was quiet for a while. Jess looked at Sam. He looked preoccupied.

"What is it, Sam?"

"Just thinking about these murders. I'm stymied. I hope Frank came up with something while we were away."

Fascinated with Sam's work, Jess never tired of hearing about his cases. He often shared his ideas with her, and she knew he liked to hear her opinion. From the first moment they met, his openness and easy communication impressed her. Another plus for a life partner.

"Do you have any theories you'd like to talk about?"

"Well, it all comes back to abused kids. It's almost as though the killer is on a vendetta. But we can't find any promising leads so far."

"You must have some."

"Yes, his description—dark, thick glasses and baseball cap—and no car seems to be involved, so he follows his victims on foot. The scenes are all within walking distance of each other."

"And it all happened in my neighborhood."

"Yes, that's why I want you to be extra careful."

"I will and I want you to be careful too. I don't want to lose you."

"Not a chance sweetheart.

CHAPTER 23

At dusk, the Avenger waits within sight of the building and sees a car in front. It is a week night and very few people exit. The mark appears. Still wearing his flowing robes and talking to a small boy. The boy gives him what appears to be a book and then waves goodbye as he enters the waiting vehicle. The priest watches the moving car, and The Voice tells The Avenger to keep to the plan. The Avenger nods and follows the mark to the rectory.

***

Reverend Alan Simpson always wanted to be a priest. His parents were devout Catholics and Alan enjoyed being in church. When his dream was realized and when he entered the priesthood, it was everything he thought it would be. Why is it so wrong to want to nurture and care for these children? I've helped them. No one seems to understand.

He then proceeded toward his living quarters at the rectory. What a nice young man. He will make a fine priest. I'm looking forward to tutoring him in the way the priest lives and serves. He dropped the book he was holding. He bent over to get it and after he straightened up, he heard a pop. On his way down again, he fell to his knees and felt the pain.

CHAPTER 24

The following week, Sam and Jess were both working long hours and had to be satisfied with phone conversations at the end of each day. When things eased up, Jess asked, "How about an early dinner tomorrow night? Brenda and Mark would like to join us. Is it all right?"

"I'd rather be alone with you."

"Me too, but Brenda asked and I hate to say no. We'll go early and make it a short evening. Then maybe we'll have some time afterward."

"Okay, I'll stop by your place around 4:30."

Sam left work early to go home, shower and look really good for Jess. He even put on a tie and sports jacket.

When she opened the door, Jess couldn't help thinking how hot Sam looked. That smile and a jacket and tie no less. She greeted him with a prolonged kiss until Sam asked, "Shall we cancel?"

She jumped away. "No, I promised Brenda we'd

meet them."

The corners of his mouth pointed down and with his shoulders slumped, "If I have to."

They met Mark and Brenda at the restaurant and since it had just opened for dinner, they were seated right away. Sam picked up the menu. "What's good here?"

Brenda said she liked the grouper, Mark, the shrimp and Jess, the salmon.

"So, are you trying to tell me it's fish?"

"Good guess."

While having dessert, and sampling each other's dishes, they asked Sam his professional opinion on the chef's expertise and he approved wholeheartedly. "This cheesecake is the best I've had in a long time. The last piece I had was super creamy and drizzled with fresh berries."

Jess asked, "Which restaurant?"

"Chez Wesley of course."

"Not that you're prejudiced."

They were enjoying themselves. Sam said to Brenda and Mark, "I forgot how nice your company is. Glad Brenda suggested it."

Mark piped up, "I feel the same. So, Sam what have you been doing with yourself?"

Jess thought no stammer.

Sam answered between bites. "As you've heard, Jess and I spent a wonderful few days in Savannah and then we've both been swamped with work."

"How about those unsolved murder cases."

"Frank is doing a lot of background checks on several suspects, but, I'm afraid he'll probably come up empty. I've been investigating house burglaries; a domestic battery; store robbery—all those fun things. They take a lot of time. And then the on-and-off investigation of those recent murders. What have you been doing?

Brenda and Mark exchanged smiles. He said, "Well, I got a promotion at work. The best part is I'll be getting more money. Now maybe I'll be able to plan our future."

Jess and Sam didn't miss the word our, they smiled at each other, and Sam lifted his wine glass. "So, this is a celebration. A toast to your bright and happy futures."

They clicked glasses. Then Jess said, "Are we celebrating anything else? Hmmm?"

Mark got red and stammered. "Nnnnnot now. MMaybe soon."

After they clicked and drank again, Mark said, "Brenda talked me into going back to Father Simpson's church."

"What did you think?"

"As usual, his sermon impressed me, but I can't get to like him. I keep thinking about the ppoor pparents who placed their trust and ffaith in him to mmentor their children. He betrayed their ttrust. I don't want to go there anymore, and may I add, Richard feels the ssame way."

Jess heard the stammer again.

Brenda said. "If you feel that strongly, Mark, maybe we'll hunt up another church that we both like."

"Thanks. I think I'd like that."

Sam had mixed feelings about religion. "I think it's great that you both feel comfort in your faith. It works for you and that's good. I think it's different for everyone. I, myself, am a product of a mixed marriage and don't participate in any traditional religion. I believe in God and in being a moral human being. That's what my parents instilled in me and it works."

Jess and Sam had never discussed religion before. Jess said, "My parents were Unitarians, but I haven't been to church for quite a while and haven't thought about it, but I feel the same way."

Sam said, "Are you serious?"

"Yes, I am. I don't have to worship God in a building. I've always spoken to Him wherever I happened to be."

Sam wanted to make something else clear. "No matter what any of us think about religion, I think we agree the leaders of all religions should have impeccable morals and be shining examples of humanity. Anyone who doesn't live by that code is not truly religious no matter what he pretends to be.

Mark responded, "That makes perfect sense to me. And it certainly applies to Father Simpson."

The conversation turned to lighter subjects and

the evening ended early. After they said their good-byes, Sam whispered to Jess, "Boy, have I missed you. I can't stand being away from you for days. I think we should live together. What do you think?"

Jess gasped. She couldn't help herself, "Live together? I don't know, Sam, this is a complete surprise! I love you and want to be with you, but I need to think about it. Can I let you know?"

"Of course. I didn't mean to spring it on you like this, it just came out."

"You know, Sam, I suddenly don't feel so well. I think I'm coming down with something. I'm sorry."

"Jess, I love you so much. Please forgive me for being so abrupt. You should get some rest. I'll see you tomorrow."

"Thanks for understanding." Jess rested her head on the seat and they drove home saying very little.

After a quick kiss at the door, she ran to the bathroom and threw up. I thought this only happened in the morning.

Jess deep in thought chomped on some dry crackers. Live with him? Do I want that for our future? I don't want to lose him. What should I do? I'll take a walk. That always clears my head. She grabbed her cell phone and went out the door.

She decided to go her usual walk route. The balmy evening and the beauty of the silhouettes of the palm trees against the darkening sky soon made her feel better.

I hope I didn't sound too short with him. He

looked so hurt. It broke my heart. I didn't know what to say. I'll have to think this through. This wasn't the proposal I was expecting.

She walked pretty fast and started to slow down as she turned the corner at the small shopping center. She cut through and then walked by the little church across the street, where Father Simpson preached. She was reminded of Mark's hint that he and Brenda are very serious. Wondered if he'd ask her to be his wife or his roommate.

I'm not being fair. When Sam finds out about the baby, he'll probably do the right thing and propose marriage. But I don't want him to feel pressured. I don't know for sure if I want to get married either. I'm so conflicted.

When Jess made the turn to go toward her building, she noticed a lone figure ahead. He seemed to be hurrying. Jess wondered who he was and continued walking. He must have heard something because he turned. Jess hid in the shadow of a palm tree. When she felt sure he didn't see her, she remembered Sam's warning but continued to follow him anyway. She was a little closer to him now and saw that he wore a baseball cap. She must be nuts. Her mind was playing tricks on her. It couldn't be the killer. She slowed down. She saw her building and he turned into the parking lot minutes before she did. He must have heard her because he turned again. There was a gun in his hand and just as Jess noticed the thick glasses and dark skin, it went off.

Jess was able to press Sam's cell phone number before she blacked out.

CHAPTER 25

"Damn, Damn, Damn," Sam screamed as he pounded the side of the steering wheel. What the hell possessed him to blurt it out like that? He wanted his proposal to be perfect. Now he ruined it. It came out all wrong. He has to fix this, and he will, he will, he will!

He felt a little better afterward but was still distressed. He ran into his apartment to get Kugel. While he waited for the dog to do his business and tried to figure out what to do, his cell phone rang.

"Hello!"

No one spoke. Sam thought this strange because not many people had his cell phone number. Just people from work, and of course, Jess. "Hello, hello." No dial tone. Jess's number was displayed. His stomach dropped.

He picked Kugel up, put him in the car and like a crazy man, drove to Jessica's.

Sam didn't see anything in the parking lot at first,

but then he approached someone lying at the side of the front entrance. He ran over and found Jess unconscious with a lot of blood flowing from her leg. He kept screaming to revive her as he pulled his tie off and used it as a tourniquet. After calling 911 and with tears rolling down his face, he kept saying, "Darling, talk to me, please talk to me. You're going to be all right. I love you. Please talk to me."

He kept this up riding to the hospital with her and while the attendants worked on her. He continued when they wheeled her into the emergency room. They told him to wait outside.

Sam's mind was a blur until an hour later, Doctor Arenstein came out. He knew him and was thankful Jess had such a good doctor.

They shook hands. "Hi Sam. I haven't seen you for a while."

"I know doc. How's my girl?"

"She lost a lot of blood, but it's good you applied a tourniquet. Now we need to get her x-rayed and into the operating room. Get the bullet out and stop the bleeding. It might be a while."

Sam sat waiting and wringing his hands. He called Frank. "Frank, Jess's in the operating room at Memorial Hospital. She was shot. I'm waiting."

"I'll be right over."

"No, please do me a favor and get my dog from the car in front of Jess's condo building. He needs to be fed and could you take care of him? Then come on over. I have to talk to you."

"I'm on my way."

Now it's getting personal. I'm going to get this son-of-a-bitch if it's the last thing I do. He alternated pacing and sitting and could hardly breathe. Please God don't punish her. It's my fault. I should have stayed with her.

When Frank arrived, he had two cups of coffee in his hands, and handed Sam one. "How is she?"

Sam shook his head from side to side. "I found her in the parking lot. Shot in the leg. I think it hit an artery. The doctor said it'd be a while." Sam tried to hold back the tears and kept dabbing his eyes and blinking.

"Sam, it's good you got her right over here. That makes all the difference. You know that! C'mon have the coffee."

"Thanks." He sat down, took the coffee and tried to breathe away the lump in his throat.

"Frank, I've been thinking. Why did this happen in her parking lot?"

Frank shrugged his shoulders.

Sam continued, "I said something to upset her. I think she went for a walk to calm herself down. She must have forgotten about my telling her she had to be extra careful. Do you think the shooter lives in her building?"

"Maybe, or he may have seen her and pretended to be walking home. When she followed him into the parking lot, he lost it."

"I want all the residents in the building interviewed, Frank."

"I'll start tomorrow. Sam, after Jess comes out of the operating room you should go home and get some rest."

"No, I'm staying here. Could you bring me a change of clothes tomorrow? Here are my keys. I'll be here until she wakes up and I know she's okay."

Frank stayed with him. Tried to make conversation. Sam just stared straight ahead. Sometimes he'd move his lips in silent prayer. Frank went to a machine and bought a couple of sandwiches, but Sam just shook his head and pushed them away.

After two hours, the doctor came out. "She's stable. We got the bullet out and were able to stop the bleeding. We placed a steel rod in the fractured femur, but she really lost a lot of blood and it'll be touch and go for a while. The baby seems to be all right, but I'm keeping her in ICU until she's out of the woods."

"The baby? She's pregnant?"

"Yes, I'd say just about one month along."

"Oh doc. Thank you very much. Can I sit with her tonight? I'll be quiet."

"Sam, normally I'd say no, but I think you know how important it is to stay out of the way. So I'll say yes for now."

"Thanks again."

Frank started to take off. "I'll be on my way. Call

144

if you need anything." He patted Sam on the back, "Congrats about the baby."

With a jolt, it hit Sam. He was going to be a father! He couldn't believe it. Why didn't she tell him? As soon as she gets better, he'll be more excited. But now he just wanted to know she'd be okay. She'll be a great mother. Oh God, please let her be all right and the baby too.

After the nurses settled her in ICU, Sam went to her. The tears started when he saw how still and pale she looked. Straining to sound calm, he talked to her. "Hi Jessica, it's me, sweetheart. I love you. You're going to be okay. I'm staying right here with you."

No wonder she was so upset. He didn't mention marriage. He asked her to live with him and it sounded as though he wanted her to be his roommate. He prayed. Please God, let her wake up soon, so I can set everything right. I'll be a good father and husband, and they'll always know how much I love them. Please don't take them away from me.

He tiptoed out of her room to make one more important call. Frank sounded drowsy when he answered. He listened to Sam's request, then turned and fell back asleep.

Sam kept his eyes on Jess for a fluttering of her eyelids or any other sign of movement, but her eyes remained closed and she was very pale.

"She looks awful. Please God help her. Don't let her die."

CHAPTER 26

The Avenger runs to a condo, locks the door and keeps the lights off.

What happened? Why was she following me? Should I have shot her? Does she know who I am?

The Avenger sits in the darkened living room and goes over the evening's events. I had to do the priest. It's part of the plan. He didn't deserve to live and keep hurting those kids.

Why did she follow me? Did she see me do it? No, I covered my tracks pretty well. Maybe it's just a coincidence.

The Avenger is up all night thinking about the next move. Did I kill her? That wasn't in the plan. But the plan is ruined anyway. The cops will be all heated up now. I should wait until things cool down.

**

Taking hold of her hand and squeezing it, Sam hoped that Jess could feel him near her. He wondered if he should call her father. No, he'll wait until she's better. No sense in worrying him now.

He'll call Brenda, though. She'd want to see Jess as soon as she could.

He looked over to see Jess still breathing with the aid of oxygen and lying under those white sheets. Sam remembered how they were all joking together just a short while ago, and Jess kidding him about his cooking. As soon as she feels up to it, he'd bring her some homemade chicken soup.

He kept thinking of these silly things to take his mind off how sick she looked. Then he remembered Sondra, and her awful final days. He cleared his throat and shook his head. No, he wouldn't think those thoughts. Only positive ones.

He thought about the night Jess laughed at herself after she fell and ruined her favorite shoes. How excited she was when she tried on the new pair and put them on right away; the day at the beach when they fell even deeper in love; the fun in Savannah and the intense lovemaking.

Oh God, don't let it happen again. Please don't take Jessica away from me too. Tell me what I can do to make her better.

The whole day passed and she lay there, not moving. Sam held her hand and silently prayed.

Frank stopped by and insisted that Sam have something to eat. They went to the cafeteria where Frank bought him some soup and a salad. Sam had a constant lump in his throat and had a hard time swallowing. His head pounded and he could hear his heart beating. He pushed the food away and stood up. "I want to go back up."

When they were in the waiting room, Frank said, "I have something to tell you."

"What is it?"

"There's been another murder."

"Who?"

"That priest, Father Alan Simpson."

"When?"

"Last night."

"Frank, do you know what this means? Jess was shot last night. Maybe she saw something?"

"I don't know but I'm on it now and you just concentrate on helping Jess get through this."

Sam tried to clear his head and think about the last time he saw Jess. At dinner with Mark and Brenda. "There's something weird here. We were just talking about this priest."

"How come?"

"Jess and a couple of friends were saying he was involved in a situation on the East Coast. Abuse of young boys. Accused but not convicted."

"How do they know that?"

"I think Jess read it in the paper."

Frank perked up. "Like the Scout leader murder. Not a father but a trusted person in contact with kids."

"We need to explore that and I keep thinking of the Memorial Hospital angle. The answer may be there. It's the same guy for sure. Did they find the slug?"

"I don't know yet."

The waiting room started to fill up. A teenage girl whose mother was in surgery, a worried couple quietly talking about their sick child, an older man waiting to hear if his wife would survive a heart attack.

Frank, about to leave, gave Sam a hug. "I'd better go. I'm going to work and I'll get back to you. Don't worry, Sam. I know she'll be fine. I just know it."

"Me too but when I see her like that it tears me in half."

Frank had interviewed some of the occupants of Jess's condo building that day but didn't mention it. Now wasn't the time. "Is there anything else I can do?"

"No, thanks, Frank. "I'm going to call Jess's partner, then I want to go back and sit with her."

"I guess I'll leave then. Call to tell me what's going on."

"I will."

Sam used his cell and called Brenda. She answered quickly. "Hi Sam. Mark told me about Jess. I've been sick with worry."

"I'm sorry I haven't called sooner but things have been crazy."

"How is she?"

"I don't really know. She lost a lot of blood and she's still in ICU." His voice caught, "Pray for her, Brenda."

"I already am. Would it be possible for me to see her?"

"They don't want visitors in ICU. They made an exception for me."

"I don't care. I'm coming anyway. I can't think of anything else."

"If you want to."

"I'll see you soon."

Sam went back and sat next to Jess's bed. He took hold of her hand again. He continued with his silent prayers until the nurse stepped in and told him someone wanted to talk to him.

He saw Brenda. "Hi, Sam. Can I just take a peek? I need to see her."

He nodded his head, looked around, and took her to see Jessica. As soon as Brenda saw her, she started to cry. He hugged her and patted her back trying to hold back his own tears. Brenda tried to reassure him. "She's very strong and she's going to come through this. I'm sure of it, Sam. We have to be strong too. She'll need us when she wakes up and we have to be encouraging and help her get better."

"You're right. We'll be strong. Thanks for coming Brenda."

"Call me if there's any change at all, please."

"I will."

Sam went back to sit with Jess. He wondered if she saw the priest murdered. That would bring them closer to solving these cases. That is if she

CHAPTER 27

The nurses kept checking Jess throughout the night and said she seemed to be breathing more normally and her blood pressure was coming up. A sense of calmness fell over Sam. He allowed his eyes to close and started to doze.

He woke to the sounds of morning activity and looked over at Jessica. She had a little more color. The doctor came in to examine her and asked Sam to leave.

When he finished, the doctor joined Sam in the waiting room with a smile on his face. "She's okay and the baby is too. I'd like her to stay in ICU for another day. Then we'll transfer her to a room."

"Is she awake?"

"Yes, you can talk to her, but not too much. She's been through a lot and is very tired. She'll want to go back to sleep."

"Thanks Dr. Arenstein."

When he saw Jessica, her eyes were half closed.

She tried to smile when she saw him. Her words were slurred. "Hi. I knew you'd come and reshcue me. Thank goodnessh for schell phones."

The floodgate of Sam's tears opened again and he said, "I'll always be there for you, and I'll never leave you." He bent over and kissed her very gently, "and that goes for our baby too."

"How'd you know?"

"Darling, you were examined from head to foot. I don't think the doctor would have missed that. Why didn't you tell me?"

"Didn't wanna tie you down."

"I'm tied down already, and I'm not complaining."

"Jessica yawned, "I'm sho happy Sham. I love you."

She closed her eyes. When Frank peeked into the room, Sam tiptoed out to talk to him and took the stuff Frank brought him. "I'm happy for you, Buddy. Good luck. I'm in the middle of getting information on the priest. We're still trying to find a connection among all the victims. Did Jess say anything about that night?"

"No, and I'm not going to ask her until she's stronger."

"I understand. When you do, tell me."

"I will. Thanks for everything, friend."

Just as Sam left the waiting room, he saw Sara and Mark. Visibly upset, Sara asked, "How is she Sam? Will she be alright?"

"Hey, thanks for coming. Yes, she's stronger and I

spoke to her for a while. She's sleeping now but no visitors allowed."

Sara breathed a deep and shaky sigh. "Oh! I'm so relieved. When can we see her?"

"Maybe tomorrow. She'll be transferred to a regular room.

Mark asked, "How are you holding up, Sam?"

"Better now. It was pretty bad there for a while."

"Yeah, you look like you haven't slept at all."

"Sitting next to her I took a few catnaps. But now, I'm invigorated."

They sat in the waiting room and continued to talk for a while.

Sam said, "Did you hear? Father Simpson was killed.

With a shocked expression, Mark said, "I can't believe it. We were talking about him at dinner! When did it happen?"

"The same night Jess got shot."

Sara asked, "Do you know who did it?"

"No, Frank's working on it. He'll keep me informed."

Mark said, "Why was Jess out that night?"

"She was annoyed with me, so I guess she wanted to walk it off. I warned her not to walk alone after dark but she did it anyway."

Mark shook his hand and patted his arm. "Keep us up to date, Sam."

Sara hugged Sam, "We'll leave now, but we'll be back soon. Take care."

After he glanced in to see Jess sleeping again, Sam took Frank's package to the men's room, washed up and changed into some fresh clothes. He shaved and stopped for a moment. He looked in the mirror. The strain of the past couple of days showed. My face looks thinner. Come to think of it my buckle moved over a notch. What a way to lose weight.

After he had a muffin and cup of coffee in the cafeteria, he went back to see Jess awake. The nurse had given her a sponge bath and combed her hair."

Sam whistled. "Well, hello beautiful. That's my girl. How do you feel?"

"Like I've been run over by a truck. But much better."

"Everyone has been asking about you and even came up to try and see you."

"Who?"

"Brenda, Sara, Mark and Frank, of course. By the way, that priest you read about, Simpson, was shot the same night you were."

"My God, we were just talking about him at dinner."

"I know. Frank is investigating both cases and wants to know what you saw that night."

"The only thing I saw was someone looking suspicious when I walked around the block. He kept looking behind and around him, so I followed him when he went into the parking lot. Then he turned around and shot me."

"What did he look like?"

"Black. Wore a baseball cap and thick glasses. Do you think it's the same guy involved in the other shootings?"

"Looks that way."

"Sam, you warned me to be very careful, and I didn't listen. I'm so sorry I put you through this."

"Sweetheart, just get better in a hurry. Nothing else matters. Sam kissed her. "That's all the business I want to talk about. Concentrate on getting stronger. Jess, have you thought about calling your father."

"Yes, but I've been thinking about how to tell him I got shot without his freaking out."

"I think you should call. He may want to be with you. I can talk to him first to assure him you're fine, and I want to ask him something anyway."

"Ask him what? You don't even know him."

"You'll find out, but first," Sam put something on her meal table. When Jessica turned to look, she saw a gleaming diamond ring in an opened velvet box. Sam got down on his knees beside her high hospital bed. "Will you marry me, Jessica Gladstone?"

CHAPTER 28

Frank stopped by Sam's place to take Kugel for a short walk. As the dog sniffed around, Frank thought about his approach during questioning this morning. After he brought Kugel in and left him food and water, Frank drove to Jess's building.

The building was six stories high with 10 condos on each floor. There are an awful lot of people here to talk to. I won't be able to finish in one day. He took out his notebook and wrote the name of the first person he was about to see. It was a brief conversation, because that man didn't even know there had been a shooting. The next didn't know anything either. Then he tried the T. Sanders' bell. A dog ran to the door, started barking and jumping on him while his mistress pulled and shouted for him to stop. She weighed at least 200 pounds and was barefoot. Wore short shorts over more-than-ample thighs. Her condo could have been very nice, but he saw a bunch of dirty dishes in the kitchen and a heap of dirty laundry in the foyer. She had a cell phone up to her ear held in place by her shoulder and was holding a full rubbish bag as she tried to get the dog to stop jumping. She talked to Frank and spoke on the phone at the same time. He interrupted her conversation to introduce himself and showed her his badge. He asked that she please hang up so he could speak to her.

"Of course," she hung up. "My mother. She has Alzheimer's and keeps asking me the same questions. Sorry about that. Can I help you? Oh, just a minute, I have to throw this rubbish down the chute."

She didn't bother to put shoes on and went out in her bare feet. When she returned, Frank started the interview, "I've come to ask you about the recent shooting of Jessica Gladstone."

"What a shock! I didn't know her very well. What's it all about?"

"That's what we're trying to find out. Did you hear or see anything unusual two nights ago?"

"No, I'm sorry. I worked late that night and came home to see the ambulance here."

"Did you know Father Alan Simpson. He preached at the church near the shopping center?"

"No. I'm sorry. I'm not very religious."

He took the name of her employer to be checked later. These were the types of answers he kept getting. No one saw or heard anything so far.

Looking at his list he saw the next name, Richard

Benson. With a deep sigh of frustration, he rang Benson's bell, announced himself and showed his ID. This condo was much neater than the previous one but very stark. He entered the near-empty living room.

Frank asked, "Did you see anything unusual the night that Jessica Gladstone was shot."

Mr. Benson appeared nervous. His left eye twitched and he looked at the floor when he spoke. "I didn't see or hear anything. How is Jess? She's a good friend of mine and I'm very concerned."

"She's improving. We're trying to find out why this happened. Since you're a friend, can you think of anyone who'd want to harm her?"

"Absolutely not. I have no idea. Maybe it was a mistake."

"Did you know Father Alan Simpson?"

"I didn't know him personally. I did attend a couple of the services at his church. I've had a problem coping with a personal problem and his sermons were inspiring. But I stopped."

"Why?"

"I heard that he molested young boys. Supposedly they cleared him, but looking at him made me feel uncomfortable."

Frank looked around the room. "You have a nice place. How long have you been here?"

"Not long. I moved here shortly after my wife died."

"So, you're retired."

"Yes, after I lost her, I needed a change, so I left the firm I worked for and moved. My wife and I planned to retire in Florida anyway. I just came down earlier."

Frank observed that he opened and closed his fists while he spoke. "Mr. Benson, you seem to be on edge. Is something the matter?"

"No, it's just so disturbing that someone almost died here. He may have shot anyone that happened to be in his way. It could have been me!"

"Mr. Benson, where were you when the shooting occurred?"

"I had just come from the airport when I saw the ambulance."

"Where were you?"

"Visiting my son in North Carolina."

"Can I have his phone number?"

"He doesn't have a phone. He's autistic and lives in a community home. I can give you that number, but I don't think it would be much use. My son's pretty content just staying in his room by himself and doesn't use their living room much. He rarely socializes. They knew I was there but didn't keep track of me every minute."

"I'd like their number anyway. Just for the record."

"Certainly."

While waiting for Richard to get the information, Frank looked around the condo. A complete opposite from the last one he visited. Freshly painted and very neat with no personal pictures. Frank wondered why he didn't display a picture of his son.

When Benson returned, he gave Frank the number and address, Frank gave him his card, "If you can think of anything, please call me."

The next person interviewed, Emily Hagan, a tall and very thin woman had thick makeup on and a sickening smile. In a Southern accent, she asked, "Hi y'all. Can I help you?"

Frank showed her his badge and asked if he could come in.

"Of course."

He noted that this condo looked completely different from the other ones he saw. It looked very modern with what appeared to be very expensive furniture.

"You have a very nice place here."

"Thank y'all. Would you like to look around?"

"Yes."

She showed him the various improvements she had made. With special pride she pointed out, "I changed the location of all the sinks. "Cause nobody wants to see a sink when they look into a room. I moved all the plumbing around."

"Hmm what a good idea!" Frank thought that this woman had some sort of a sink fetish.

"I decided to streamline the kitchen and cut down on the number of cabinets. All those pots and pans are really unnecessary. I don't cook much anyway."

Frank commented, "Everything is very nice." Then he asked, "How well did you know Ms. Gladstone?"

"Well, I'm sorry she was shot, but I didn't like her too much."

"Why?"

"She's on the condo board, and not very nice. When our lobby was being redecorated, she switched the choice of the flooring at the last minute without tellin' anyone. She and the flooring salesman were in cahoots and changed the purchase order while they were ridin' up on the elevator."

"I see." Frank had never heard of a flooring conspiracy before and he doubted that it really happened. "Is there anything else you don't like about her?"

"She thinks she's so high and mighty and important."

"Why do you think that?"

"I just know it."

"Can you tell me where you were the night Ms. Gladstone was shot?"

"Out shoppin'. I like to shop later to avoid the crowds. Our market is open 'till 10 o'clock."

"Can anyone confirm that's what you did?"

"My, am I a suspect?" with a giggle.

"Everyone is, ma'am, until we find out who did this."

"I did talk to the lady who passes out food samples at the market. I don't know her name, but she's always there."

"Okay. Thank you."

As he followed her to the door, he noticed that her body slanted to the right. He thought she must have some kind of spinal column problem.

The next several people he spoke to didn't come up with anything relevant. Frank looked at his notebook. From all those names, he'd say that so far there are two people of interest: Richard Benson and Emily Hagan. But he'll have to come back and interview people he didn't speak to. Probably more than one time.

When Frank got home, his house was a mess. Throw pillows were ripped apart, the curtains were pulled down, stuff on his desk was on the floor. At first, he thought there was an intruder, and he looked around from room to room with his gun drawn. The robbers were probably disappointed, they didn't find anything valuable here. Looks like they took their anger out on my furnishings.

Then he saw Kugel in the middle of Frank's bed among a sea of shredded foam rubber. He had a pillow in his mouth and was shaking it from side to side. When he spotted Frank, he jumped down and ran over and rubbed against his leg whining. Frank bent down and picked him up, "Oh baby. You're homesick and you miss your daddy, don't you? I'll bring you home tomorrow."

CHAPTER 29

When Jessica saw the ring, she thought, I'm really sick. Now I'm hallucinating. She heard Sam's voice coming from the floor. And I'm hearing things. She felt very weak, "Sam, I can't see you. Where are you?"

"Down here. I just asked you to marry me."

"You did?"

Sam stood up and made a face when he heard his knees creak. "Yes, I did." He reached for the ring and put it on her finger.

"Oh yes, Sam. I'll marry you. Can we do it before the baby comes?"

He laughed, "Whenever you want sweetheart." He tried to maneuver himself around her raised leg and hanging liquids so he could kiss her.

"Oh, I feel so happy, but I ache all over. We may have to wait a while. When did you buy this gorgeous ring?"

"The day of Mark's birthday party. I wanted to

give it to you at just the right moment, and this is it. You don't have the strength to refuse me."

"Oh Sam, you're crazy."

"I'm crazy in love and as soon as you're up to it, let's call your father."

She started to get drowsy, "We will, but I'm a little tired now. Can I take a nap first?"

"You close your eyes and I'll be here when you wake up. I love you, Jessica."

"I love you too, Shham." She slurred, and she was already asleep.

Sam tiptoed out of the room and saw Jess's doctor at the nurse's station. "Hi Dr. Arenstein, can I talk to you for a minute?"

"Of course."

"I just want you to know, I asked Jessica to marry me, and she said yes."

The doctor pumped Sam's hand enthusiastically. Congratulations! I'm very happy for both of you."

"Thank you. What's her status now? She seems really tired."

"That's normal considering what she's gone through. She's much improved and will be transferred out of ICU this afternoon. Long range, she'll have to be off her feet and on crutches while her fracture heals. She's pretty healthy generally, so with the aid of physical therapy, I predict it will be around 6 to 8 weeks before she can bear any weight on that leg and 4 months or so before she can return to regular activities."

"What about the baby?"

"Fortunately, the obstetrician determined that the baby is all right. However, we have to use precautions if she has to have any x-rays during her pregnancy."

Sam took a long breath. "Thanks. I'd appreciate your keeping me up to date on her progress."

"Of course."

After leaving the doctor, Sam took out his cell and called Brenda. "She's out of the woods and will be in a room later on. I'm sure you can see her briefly tomorrow."

"I'm so looking forward to seeing her. Thanks for calling me, Sam."

Then he spoke to Frank. "Jess is feeling much better and will be in a regular room soon. It's time I got briefed on what's been happening but I still want to hang around here today. Tonight I'll probably go home to sleep. I'll let you know when I'll be there."

"I'm happy about Jess. By the way Kugel is there already. He was homesick and I brought him back. He's okay though. I stopped in to feed and walk him."

"Homesick? How can you tell if a dog is homesick?"

"Trust me. I could tell."

"See you soon."

When Sam went back to Jess, she was awake. Nurses and attendants were getting her ready to be moved. He got near enough to tell her, "I'm going to stay out of the way, but I'll follow you up to your room."

She smiled broadly, "You mean, as they say in police lingo, you've got my back?"

"You're damn right."

He watched from the doorway while two nurses settled Jess in bed. He said a silent prayer. Thank you, God, for not letting Jess die.

The head nurse smiled at him, "She developed a nice rock on her finger. Lots of luck to you both. You can go in now."

Her new room was much better than ICU. Bright and sunny with Sam's roses and the flowers sent by Brenda arranged so Jess could see them from her bed.

Sam bent over and kissed her, "Are you feeling stronger?"

"Much stronger. They're going to get me to take a one-legged step soon."

"So, shall I get Dad on the phone?"

"OK. But I want to talk to him first."

She took Sam's phone and punched in her father's number. "Hi Daddy, it's Jess."

"Hello sweetheart, how are you?"

"How's Maggie?"

"She's great. We just came back from our walk. What's new with you?"

"Well, I had a little accident and I'm in the hospital, but I'm fine now."

"What happened?"

Jess proceeded to tell him as gently as she could and before she finished, her father interrupted her, "We're coming down there. I'm going to call right after I hang up and make reservations. We'll stay until you're on your feet."

"Oh Daddy, I want to see you, but you don't have to do that."

"Yes, I do."

"One other thing, remember I told you I met a wonderful man? Well, we fell in love. You're going to love him too. He wants to talk to you."

He answered suspiciously, "Put him on."

"Hello Mr. Gladstone. My name is Sam Wesley and I love your daughter very much and want to be with her for the rest of my life. I've asked her to marry me and would like your blessing."

"Wow! That's a lot of information for me to digest. So, you want my permission?"

"No, she already said yes, but I do want your blessing."

"I think I like you already, but since she's my only daughter, I'll have to reserve that decision until we've met."

"It's a deal. Please let me know when your plane lands, and I'll pick you up."

"I will, and, Sam, take care of my girl until we get there."

"It will be my privilege."

After giving Jess's father his cell number, he hung

up and looked over at Jess. She beamed. "You always know just the right thing to say."

"You're a lucky woman," he bent over and kissed her again. "How about let's have dinner together and then I'm going home to let you get a good night's sleep."

"Good. You really look like you need some rest."

"But handsome anyway, right?"

"Right."

They both had a hospital meal together and Jess's appetite was reasonably good but on the way home Sam planned to fulfill the promise he made to himself, When I get home, the first thing I'm going to do is make her some chicken noodle soup. Then I'll call Frank.

Sam stopped by the market to get the soup fixings and after greeting and playing with Kugel for a while, he started to put together his Superb Soup.

He spoke out loud to his mother, "A 'bowl of health' for my wife-to-be. You'd love her, Mom. I wish you could be here to meet her."

When the soup simmered on the stove, he called Frank.

"I'm home, c'mon over and I'll let you share some of Jessica's chicken soup."

He prepared a salad while waiting for Frank to arrive, "Now this is what I call real food, as opposed to hospital Jello."

CHAPTER 30

Frank appeared at Sam's door wearing shorts and a tee—holding his briefcase. He saluted. "Frank Romano, reporting for duty."

Sam did a double take—surprised that Frank dressed so casually. Unlike Sam, he almost never wore shorts. "Don't you look fuckin' sporty."

"You mean sloppy. I decided to fit in with your mode of dress this evening."

"Very funny. C'mon let's go to the kitchen for food."

After Sam and Frank finished eating, they cleared off the table. Frank carefully spread out his notes on what he found out at the condo building and information on the Father Simpson murder.

"I interviewed some of the parishioners at Simpson's church. He seemed to have kept his problem under control since being here. They all had high praise for him and were shook up that someone had killed him."

Sam shook his head, "I think the Simpson murder happened just before Jess got shot. If we can find out who shot her, we've got our perp."

"I agree. So far, I have a few people of interest at the condo building who might know something but are afraid to say."

"Who?"

"One who tries real hard to sound sincere, but she doesn't ring true. Her name is Trixie Sanders. By the way, she doesn't look anything like her name. She's a very—shall we say abundant woman. Dresses as though she were a woman half her size, and not a pretty sight. She says she saw nothing that night because she came home from work after the fact, and she doesn't know the priest. There's really nothing concrete there, but we may want to talk to her again."

Kugel came pattering into the room and nuzzled against Sam's leg. "Who else?"

"A nutcase, Emily Hagan, who didn't like Jess. She didn't seem very sorry about the shooting, but I don't think she saw anything. She didn't know about the priest at all. I think she's just a typical complainer and sick in the head. Then there's Richard Benson."

"He's Jess's neighbor."

"Yeah, he said he and Jess are friends. But when we were talking, he appeared to be nervous and uncomfortable. I guess he's got a son who's autistic and lives in North Carolina. Benson's alibi is a little shaky. If he weren't Jess's friend, I'd say he'd be a perfect candidate for a second look. We might want to anyway."

Sam started to load the dishwasher. "Okay. Say, did you finish checking backgrounds of the record people at Memorial Hospital? Maybe we can find something there."

"I'm almost done. I stopped because I wanted to start on the condo residents."

"Makes sense, but when you finish with all the condo people, let's get back to the Memorial Hospital stuff."

"Will do."

"Since Jess is feeling better, I'll be able to get back to work soon and start to pull my weight again."

Frank chuckled, "It's about time."

"She'll need help when she gets home, so I'm picking up her folks tomorrow. They want to stay with her. That'll set my mind at ease, and I'll be able to get back to work. But I want to be available to drive her to appointments or anything else I need to do. By the way, I asked her to marry me."

Frank screamed, "Yahoo!" and hurried over to shake Sam's hand. "And you're just telling me now?"

"I don't think I believe it yet."

Frank patted his back and gave him a hug, "Well, congratulations! Have you talked about a wedding date yet?"

"Not yet. She has a lot of recuperating to do first."

"Boy, you're a busy guy. A wife and a baby. A nice

package."

"I'm a lucky man. Frank. Please keep the baby news under wraps for now."

"Of course, Sam. Married! Obviously, she hasn't found out any of your faults yet.

"We'll keep those to ourselves, shall we?"

"Maybe yes, maybe no. I'll see."

"Frank, seriously, I appreciate your taking over this investigation by yourself since the shooting."

"What are partners for? You'd do the same for me."

"Let's hope I never have to."

They continued to talk for a couple of hours—about the cases and his engagement. When Frank left, Sam leaned against the door. Frank's a good friend. It's nice to have someone to talk to. He's always there during the good times and the bad. I only hope he finds someone who'll make him as happy as Jess makes me. If that were possible.

He started to feel the effect of very little sleep the last couple of days. He was in the shower when the phone rang and felt a tinge of worry. He hoped nothing went wrong with Jess, so he got out, creating a dripping wet trail and rushed to answer.

"Hello Sam, this is Tom Gladstone, Jess's father."

A sigh of relief. "Hi. Good to hear from you again. Did you get those reservations?"

"I did, but before we talk about all that. Man to man, please tell me exactly what happened and what Jessica's condition is."

Sam understood Mr. Gladstone's concern for his daughter and reassured him that Jess would be fine. Sam felt good about him. I know we'll get to be great friends. It'll be nice to have a close family again. Sam didn't say anything about the baby. He thought Jess would want to tell him herself.

Sam got all the flight information. "I'll see you both tomorrow and bring you right to the hospital.

"Thanks, I'll feel better when I see her. And, Sam, congratulations. You have my blessing. I can tell Jess made the right choice and you'll be good to my little girl. Right?"

"You have my sacred promise."

Just before bed, Frank padded into the kitchen to prepare Jess's soup for delivery. Mr. Gladstone is a good guy. If I have a daughter, I want to be a father like him.

Sam allowed himself to dream a little. A daughter would be nice. I want her to look just like Jess and have her personality. Although a son would be great too. We could do lots of stuff together. Of course, either our son or daughter will be brilliant. God, I never dreamed I could be so happy.

He added the noodles to the soup, I wonder if it'll be a girl or a boy? Should we know ahead of time or would Jess want to be surprised? I guess it's too early to ask her.

CHAPTER 31

When Frank returned to Jess's condo building he walked by the spot where Sam found her. There are 60 condos in this building. There must be at least one person who saw something relevant.

Frank started to sneeze. He knew why when he saw a couple of magnolia trees at either end of the building. In addition to the kumquat trees and plantings at the entrance, the landscaping of the building was beautiful. However, the blooming magnolia trees' fragrance permeated the area. Why did I decide to live in this state? I sneeze most of the time. Guess it's probably better than the horrible weather and treacherous driving. Maybe I'll see an allergist.

Early morning people were coming out and heading toward their cars. Better get started before all of them go off for the day.

He took the elevator up to the fifth floor and rang Mark Janus's bell. When he opened the door,

Frank sized him up. Good looking young man. Built well and dressed in a casual sport shirt and slacks.

"Good morning, Mr. Janus, I'm Frank Romano, one of the detectives investigating the shooting incident involving Jessica Gladstone."

"I was jjust on mmy way tto wwork."

Surprised by his stammer, Frank said, "I don't think this will take too long."

"Okay. Cc'mon in. I'll be right back."

Frank heard the water running and wondered if he was one of those obsessive compulsives who wash their hands a lot.

When Mark returned. "JJess is a friend of mmine, I'll be happy to ddo what I can. What have you found out so far?"

"Nothing worth mentioning. We're still talking to everyone. I have just a few questions. Where were you that night?"

"I had a tough day at wwork and came home with a tterrible headache, so I went to bed early."

"Did you see or hear anything unusual?"

"Nno, as I ssaid. I was sleeping."

"Do you get headaches frequently."

"Well, I have a high pressure jjob, so I do have them often."

Frank looked around Mark's condo. Very neat and clean. Unusual for a single guy. "This is a nice place. How long have you lived here?"

"Just a few mmonths. I sstill have to bbuy more

ffurniture. I haven't had the ttime."

"Where did you live before moving to Florida?"

"Chicago. I wworked for a ccomputer ssoftware ccompany there. They ttransferred mme to their office down here."

"What's the name of the company."

"BSO Technology Services"

"I guess you must like the weather here better too."

"I sure do. Hated the winters in Chicago. Have you sspoken to anyone else in the bbuilding?"

"I did a few days ago, but not everyone. Well Mark, thanks for now. If you think of anything else, please let me know. Here's my card."

When Frank left, he thought he'd call Chicago and do some snooping. Is Mark's speech impediment a nervous reaction? If so, why?

Frank wanted to talk to Richard Benson again. He needed to ask him another question.

At Richard's door, Frank said, "Mr. Benson. Sorry to bother you again. I have just one more question."

"What is it?"

"Could you tell me where you lived before moving to Florida?"

"Providence, Rhode Island."

"And the name of the firm you worked for?"

"John Ingram and Associates—say what's this about?"

"These are routine questions we ask everyone."

Richard's voice shook. "Is that all then?"

"Yes, thanks very much."

This guy is very edgy. Is there something he's not telling me or is it just his nature?

Several people weren't home. Frank assumed they must be working. *I'll come back. Next time in the evening.*

He reflected on his visits to the condo residents. Both Mark and Richard acted as though they were hiding something. *At least that's my impression.*

He spent the rest of the morning interviewing at Memorial and had lunch in the hospital cafeteria. *If you're not sick when you start eating here, you will be by the time you leave.*

If I could cook like Sam, I'd be a lot healthier. Maybe I'll get a pizza for dinner. That's healthy—tomatoes, cheese and pepperoni. Vegetables and protein.

After the sucky lunch, he went back to the station. Then he started looking into the backgrounds of all of the people he saw that morning. Nothing turned up during the first few calls, so he took a break and walked over to get a cup of coffee and a stale donut. *Maybe a sugar rush will help me keep going.*

The next couple of calls were more promising. He paused and put his feet up on the desk, leaned back in his chair and thought about his last conversation. *I have to get back to Sam and talk about this.* Frank didn't want to bother Sam at the hospital, so he called and left a message on Sam's home phone, "Hi Sam. It's Frank. I think I uncovered something important during my interviews today. Will talk to you about it tomorrow. Have a good night."

He worked the entire afternoon until he realized how hungry he was. I got a pretty good day's work in today. I think I'll go back to the condo building tomorrow evening." Grabbed his jacket off the hook and looked forward to having a pizza. Let's see—pepperoni or mushrooms? What the hell, both.

CHAPTER 32

Jess woke up still feeling weak but better, so she called Brenda. "Hi, partner."

"I'm so glad to hear your voice. How are you feeling?"

"Not wonderful, but pretty good, considering. How's business?"

"It's fine. Everything's under control, so you can concentrate on getting well. I called some of the staff to give me a hand for a while. I can get away this afternoon. Are you up to having me visit you?"

"Maybe tomorrow. I still sleep a lot and I'd be lousy company. But I have a surprise."

"Guess."

"Cut it out, Jess. What?"

"Sam proposed."

Brenda screamed, and Jess shook her head and moved the phone from her ear. "He did?"

"He sure did, and I got a gorgeous ring. I'll tell you everything when I see you."

"Can't wait. See you tomorrow. Is noon okay?"

"Yup. See you then."

What a great friend. She's genuinely happy for me. Hope Mark asks her to marry him soon. I want the same for her.

She drifted off to sleep again and when she awoke, she saw Sara. "Hi! What are you doing here?"

Sara sat at her bedside. "I couldn't wait to see you. You seem better."

"I am. Not perfect yet but I'm getting there. How are you?"

Jess tried to move over to her side a bit to feel more comfortable. A shooting pain ran through her and she couldn't help making a face.

"I'm very worried about you. I don't want to tire you out. Maybe I should go."

"No, stay a while. At least until I fall asleep again. I'm not wonderful company these days. What's new?"

"Oh, nothing. When do you think you'll be able to come home?"

"I don't know yet. I'm still shaky. I want to be able to function when I leave."

"I'll be happy to help you."

"Thanks, but my folks are on their way here, so they'll be a help and, of course, Sam." She held out her hand, showing Sara her ring.

Sara's eyes popped. "Oh! How beautiful. Congratulations! Did you set a date?"

"We haven't talked about that yet. How's Richard treating you?"

Sara got up and walked to the front of the bed. "He's okay."

"Just okay? What's the matter?"

"He's starting to get on my nerves. He's pressuring me to spend the night with him and I don't think I want to. And then there's the business with his son."

"What do you mean?"

"Well, I'm tired of hearing that he wishes the boy was normal, so he'd have a buddy and do all kinds of things with him. Says some parents don't know how lucky they are. They take their normal kids for granted and ignore them or yell at them or even worse hit them. Then he gets depressed and the whole night gets ruined."

Jess felt sorry for Sara and felt some responsibility for what she was going through. After all, she did introduce them.

"Have you tried talking to him?"

"Yes, but he won't listen. Says that sometimes the boy ignores him when he visits. Mark thinks I should stop seeing him and I might. But, why am I bothering you about this? You should get your rest."

"I wish I had an answer."

"So do I. Anyway, I'm going now. Wanted to see for myself that you're okay. I'll be back when you're stronger."

"Call me, Sara, and thanks for coming."

When Sam got to the hospital later that morning, he saw Jessica sitting up. The nurse helped her stand with crutches. She took two small hops, and then sat in a chair. When she saw Sam, "What do you think? Am I ready for the Olympics?"

"Without a doubt, honey. He bent down, kissed her and patted her tummy. By the way I brought you some chicken noodle soup. The nurse put it in the fridge for lunch if you want it."

"Want it? I can't wait. What time is it now?"

"Okay, it's lunch time. I'll go get it."

Sam pulled his chair close to the bed and watched her gobble up the soup. She told him about Sara's visit.

"What does her son think about all this?"

"Mark thinks she should stop dating Richard."

"That's too bad. They were good together for a while. Maybe it'll all work out."

"Maybe."

Sam stood and kissed her. "And now I gotta go meet your folks at the airport."

"Okay, and Sam be on your best behavior. I want them to like you."

"I'll try. Oh, your dad called me last night to ask all about your condition. I assured him that you're doing fine but didn't want to tell him about the baby. I figured you'd want to do that in your own time."

"Good. I want to see his face when he hears he's

going to be a grandfather!"

Sam grabbed her left hand. "I was right. It looks great on your finger."

"And I'm never taking it off."

"Anyway, I'm going." He kissed her again. This time with a little more emotion and with his hand sliding down her back.

"Do you have to leave right this minute?"

"Why, what do you have in mind?"

"Very funny. As if you could navigate with the contraption holding up my leg."

"This is a conversation for another time. Bye."

"See ya."

Sam was so pleased she was doing a lot better. Almost back to her old self. He was a little nervous waiting for Mr. and Mrs. Gladstone. They were scheduled to arrive any minute and he wondered how he'd know them. He'd soon find out. They were starting to unload.

No problem. Sam saw an older couple looking around and Sam went over and asked, "Mr. and Mrs. Gladstone?"

"Yes, and you're Sam." Mr. Gladstone shook hands and Maggy, very pretty and with a pleasant smile, hugged him.

He liked them already. They walked toward the baggage pickup and spoke as though they were old friends.

"How's my girl?"

"She's wonderful. I just saw her, and she got out

of bed for a while. She's very excited to see you both."

"The weather is much warmer here," Mrs. Gladstone observed. "I hope I didn't pack clothes that are too hot. We were in such a rush; we threw things in the suitcases."

"If there's a problem, I can take you shopping and show you where the closest mall is."

Her dad said, "I want to see Jessica now. Do you think it's okay if we go right to the hospital."

"Of course. We're on our way."

On the ride over, Sam saw how worried her father looked. "Don't worry, Mr. Gladstone, Jess is much better."

"What a nightmare. You never think this could happen to your child."

"I agree. It's awful. But she's on the mend and as soon as she heard you were coming, she perked right up. You're her best medicine."

When Jess saw them, the three of them hugged and they all talked at once. Teary-eyed, Mr. Gladstone kept patting Jess's hair and kissing her head. "You look pretty good. I didn't know what to expect."

Jessica pointed to Sam, "What, no kiss?"

"Oh, I guess so" and he shuffled toward her.

"I feel so much better. Dad, Maggie, see my ring!"

They made all the appropriate sounds and then Jessica said, "I guess a girl's got to go to extreme measures to get this guy to finally pop the question."

"You didn't have to go that far, honey." Her father commented.

"Did you guys get to know each other?"

Sam answered, "Yes, and guess what? Dad approves."

"I knew he would." And she put out her arms for another hug from her father.

CHAPTER 33

The Avenger hides in the bushes at the side of the parking lot. Not a long wait before the prey leaves the police station and starts walking down the steps and into the pizza parlor next door. Through the window, The Avenger watches the conversation between the victim and the man behind the counter. Carrying his box out the door, he hesitates but then continues to walk toward his car.

***

Frank felt pretty good about making some headway at work and went to the pizza parlor; a lightness in his step and swinging his brief case. After entering the restaurant, he smelled the pizza Mike was making and could almost taste it.

Mike asked, "How's it going?"

"Not bad, but I could use a pepperoni and mushroom pizza to make me even better."

"Coming up, it'll take a few minutes."

"Fine, how's the family?"

"Good, and how's yours?"

"They're good. Both my girls are in college now."

"They're getting big, huh?"

"Sure are. Haven't seen them for a while 'cause I've been so busy. Think I'll call them tonight."

Mike handed Frank the hot box. "Here you go. Enjoy the pizza. See you next time."

"So long."

Mike glanced out the window and saw Frank entering the parking lot. Frank waved to him and put his nose near the box breathing in the delicious smell. While he walked toward is car, Frank had a strange feeling someone was behind him. He stopped and listened. Didn't hear anything. Probably his imagination.

He continued to walk. Again, he thought someone was there. In one move, Frank reached for his gun and turned. Before pulling the trigger, he felt every cop's nightmare.

Mike saw a skirmish in the lot and thought he heard a shot. He saw someone running away, holding a brief case. Mike called 911 and ran to see if he could help.

CHAPTER 34

Richard Benson, a 65-year-old, man had been a successful lawyer with a large firm in Providence, R.I. Life was perfect. He loved his wife very much. Had a good marriage. They were happy until his son, Jimmy, was diagnosed as being autistic. They had to send him to a community home where he would have a more productive life. Richard's wife helped him cope with their situation, and until she got sick and died, he was able to come to terms with their lot in life. But then he lost it. His moods were erratic at work and eventually they asked him to leave.

He retired and came to Sarasota, Florida hoping the change of scenery would help his state of mind. He sees his son every other weekend and tries to enjoy the visits but always comes back with a heavy heart. He knows Jimmy's autism will never change, and he should accept and love him, but Richard still has a tough time dealing with it. At times the loss of both his wife and his son's condition is too much to handle.

Volunteering for several organizations keeps him busy. He does pro bono legal work for the elderly, works in a soup kitchen and is a Big Brother to Paul, a 13-year-old boy. Today, they went to a basketball game and then out for a hamburger. His son is grown now, but Richard couldn't help thinking about him at Paul's age. Paul's father is dead, and sometimes Richard finds himself pretending the boy is his own and enjoying all the normal things 13-year-olds do. He thinks Paul pretends too.

But when Richard returns home from his Big Brother activities, and thinks of all the fathers who don't appreciate their boys, depression sets in.

Jess's shooting unhinged him. He likes her and told the detective so. Why did he return to talk to him that day?

When he met Sara Janus, he started to enjoy life more. But lately, he reverted to his gloomy thoughts about Jimmy. Talking to Sara helped. But the last time he spoke to her, she seemed to be getting tired of his complaining.

I don't want to lose her. She's right. I've got to get over myself. He reached for the phone. "Hello Sara, are you busy?"

"No. Why?"

"I've been thinking about our last conversation and you're right. I'm getting on with my life. So, I'd like to invite you to a special evening. Are you interested?"

"I don't know. What do you mean?"

"Dinner and dancing at the Colby Hotel. Their food is great and the band is fantastic. Besides, we haven't gone dancing yet."

"You know, Richard, I think that would be fun. But better still, why don't we have a quiet dinner in one of their plush rooms."

"Oh Sara. That would be wonderful!"

"Why don't I meet you there after work on Friday?"

"I'm looking forward to it. I'll make the reservations."

Richard hung up. That was easier than I thought.

CHAPTER 35

Jess's parents and Sam stayed with her most of the afternoon. When she told her dad about the baby, he said, "Oh M'God, I'm going to be a grandfather! Be prepared to see us more often. We want to see our grandchild grow up."

Maggie said, "I can't wait. Maybe we could rent a place for the winter and babysit. I'm dying to hold a baby in my arms again."

Jess laughed. "Whoa. First, I'd love it, but only if you promise not to spoil the little thing. And let's keep all those ideas on hold until the kid gets born."

Her father agreed. "You're right. It's just such wonderful news, it's hard not to be excited."

They were all talking at once. Sam sat back and enjoyed watching, but Jess started to get tired. "Honey, we're going to leave now. You get some sleep. I'll get your parents settled in the condo, and we'll be back tomorrow and talk some more."

Sam kissed Jess, held her face in both his hands

and looked into her eyes. "You're looking like my old Jess again."

"What do you mean old?"

After her parents hugged and kissed Jess, her father said, "Now, you have a good night. We'll be back before you know it."

***

Sam had already stocked Jessica's fridge with food and when they arrived at her place, he said, "You unpack and I'll rustle up something for dinner."

He made a large Caesar salad, baked potatoes, steamed some string beans and put steaks under the broiler. He didn't have time to make dessert, so he bought a cheesecake at his favorite market. They were ravenous and the Gladstones marveled at how Sam prepared dinner so fast. At dessert and coffee, Mr. Gladstone said, "Our reservations were made for one way. We intend to stay until Jess is well on her way to fend for herself."

Sam breathed a sigh of relief, "I hoped you'd say that. I need to get back to work, but I'll be helping as much as I can—take her to doctor's appointments or anywhere she needs to go. I'm planning to have someone come in every day to cook and clean, but my mind will be more at ease knowing you're here, and I know Jess will be happy."

Sam wanted them to relax while he cleaned up, but they both insisted on helping. While the three of them worked, Jess's father told Sam about Jess's childhood. He liked hearing how mischievous she was as a kid. I wonder if the baby will be like her? Then Sam's cell rang.

It was his supervisor. "Sam! Some bad news. Frank was shot!"

Sam slid down the side of the counter. "Shit! You're kiddin' me. What happened?

CHAPTER 36

Dreading the answer, Sam asked, "Is Frank dead?"

"No, but he has a gunshot wound in the head and they don't know how extensive it is or if he'll make it."

"Damn it, where is he now?"

"At Memorial Hospital."

"I'll be right there."

Jess's parents were in the kitchen and overheard Sam's conversation. Her dad asked, "What happened?"

"My partner is hurt. I have to get down to the hospital. I'm sorry to leave like this."

"It's okay. We'll be fine. If you need to attend to things, we can take a cab to the hospital tomorrow."

"I'll be in touch."

He rushed out of the condo and drove like a madman with the flashing light on the roof.

He's got to be all right. He's a great cop and a

great guy. We've been a team for a long time. He's not just a partner, we support each other. After Sondra died, he was there for me, and during his divorce, we talked and talked. He's family, and I fuckin' will get the guy who shot him.

Sam's vision was hampered by the tears starting to form and he shook them off. *I hope I get there in time. What am I saying? He'll be all right.*

He screeched into emergency parking, slammed on the brakes and ran into the hospital.

He took out his badge and asked, "Where's Frank Romano? And who's his doctor?"

On his way to get more information, he saw his supervisor, Jim Seavey, in the waiting room.

"Tell me everything."

"We have an eyewitness. He owns the pizza parlor next to the station's parking lot. Saw a guy running from the scene carrying something—a black guy wearing a baseball cap. He ran to see what was going on and found Frank with blood pouring from his head and partially conscious. Frank said, 'same guy.' Oh, and he saw Frank's gun on the ground."

"What did the doctor say?"

"He's in surgery now. We'll know more after."

"I'm calling his ex-wife. His daughters should know. They'll want to be here."

He checked his book for Frank's emergency numbers and called Rhode Island. He tried to assure them the best he could, but suggested they come right away. They said they'd come and got

Sam's number so he could pick them up after they land.

After his call, Sam checked his voicemails. He said to his boss, "Frank left a voice mail at my house, saying after he did some background checks, he discovered something important about our case. He said he'd tell me about it tomorrow."

"Do you think the shooter knew what he found out?"

"Yuh, but how?"

"Somehow the perp knew Frank could have found out something new during an interview. We need to find out who Frank questioned yesterday.

Jim glanced at his watch. "Let's hope he can tell us himself. It's been a couple hours. I think we'll be here a long time."

"In that case, I'm going up to see Jess. To tell her what's going on."

Sam rode the elevator up to Jess's floor. She was watching TV. "Hi, beautiful."

"What are you doing back here? I didn't expect to see you until tomorrow."

"I know, but I need to tell you something."

"Are my folks all right?"

"They're just fine. It's Frank. He was shot and is in surgery now."

"Oh no! Will he be OK?"

Sam's voice broke. "God Jess, I hope so. It doesn't look good. Frank is like a brother to me. I don't know what I'd do if he doesn't make it."

Jess held out her arms. "Come here."

They held each other. "He'll make it. We'll both pray and believe. He'll come through; I know he will. Look at me. I wasn't so great. Think of me then and look at me now."

"I hope you're right. We won't know anything until he's out of the operating room. I'll call you as soon as I know. I want to get back down there. He can come out of surgery any time now."

He kissed her lips. Then stood up, pulled up the covers and kissed her belly. "You guys get some rest. I love you both."

When Sam got back down, his boss asked, "How's Jessica? I hear she's gonna be okay."

"It'll be a while, but she will be. Another thing— this son-of-a-bitch is getting out of control. He shoots her in the leg and Frank in the head. The other shootings were in the back."

Jim said, "Think about it. Jessica caught him by surprise and she saw what he looked like after he turned to face her, so that was a wild shot."

"Right. And Frank may have felt someone following him and drew his gun ready to fire after he turned."

"Yuh and the guy wanted to get away quick. He pulled the trigger and ran."

"Did you say the eyewitness said the shooter carried something?"

"Yup."

"Could be Frank's brief case. He was going to see

me tomorrow and knew I'd probably be either at the hospital with Jess, or at her house with Jess's parents. He wanted to bring the stuff he had with him."

They both took turns pacing and running to get coffee. At one point Sam dropped off to sleep for a couple of minutes. When he shook himself awake, he heard his boss snoring.

When the doctor came through the door, Sam's heart dropped and he and Jim jumped up to meet him.

"I've got good news. I think he'll make it. Even though the bullet struck him between the eyes, it shattered into three pieces against his skull. The fragments ran under his skin and exited through his cheek on one side of his head and near his ear on the other. We removed the fragments and stitched him up. It's a damn miracle. I've never seen anything like it."

Sam breathed a sigh of relief and asked. "Can I see him?"

"When he wakes up, but he may have trouble talking because of the wound in his cheek."

"Doctor, I need to make arrangements for him to be guarded. We won't tell anyone he's in such good shape. In fact, we'll say he's in a coma. I'm afraid the shooter will come back and try to get him. So for the time being, no one is allowed to visit except for his family. I'll talk to them about this."

The doctor said, "Okay, tell me what to do."

"Don't talk to anyone about his case, and I'll do the rest."

Sam's cell rang and after he spoke to one of Frank's daughters, he said to his boss, "I'm going to the airport to pick up his kids."

CHAPTER 37

When Jessica's parents arrived at the hospital the next day, she was on the phone talking to Sam. He told her about Frank's condition and not to tell anyone. To stick to the story that Frank's in a coma.

Her father asked, "Sam?"

"Yes."

"How's his partner?"

"They don't know yet. Right now, he's in a coma."

"Sam must be devastated."

"He is. They're very close."

Jess hated to lie, but she promised.

Her dad asked, "How are you?"

"I'm getting there."

Her parents were telling her about their night. Her dad said, "Your condo is beautiful and what a great view. And we woke up to the sounds of all kinds of birds. Nothing like New England. All we hear in the morning up North are crows."

Jess was glad that her father was so happy. At first, she resented Maggy. The usual stepmother thing. But when she got to know her, they became fast friends and understood why her father fell in love with her. She saved him from a lifetime of loneliness.

Brenda popped in and said, "Sorry I'm early, I couldn't wait anymore."

Jess said, "I'm glad."

She introduced her parents and they talked for a while. Her dad said, "As long as Brenda is here, we're going down to the cafeteria to get a cup of coffee. You want anything?"

"Nope. See you later."

After they left, Brenda said, "You look good. Are you feeling better?"

"Much. They had me up trying to use my crutches. I need more practice, but I hope I'll be able to go home soon anyway."

Jess held out her hand. "Look."

Brenda started to do a little dance—tapping her feet and moving side to side. Then gave Jess a big hug. "Congratulations! The ring's gorgeous! I bet you felt a lot better after Sam proposed."

"You're right. I have something else to tell you."

"What?"

"I'm pregnant."

"You are??" and Brenda repeated her little dance.

"Yup. Even though it was a complete surprise. I'm very happy about it."

"How come you didn't use protection?"

"We did, but you know what they say about how you're not always completely safe. Anyway, thank God the baby's still okay."

"Oh boy! I'm going to be an aunt." Brenda grabbed her and gave her another hug and kiss.

Jess offered Brenda candy from the box on her table. "So, tell me, are you busy at the office?"

"We are but it's all under control, and our accountant tells me we're doing okay. So don't you worry about anything."

"How's Mark?"

Brenda found a spot on Jess's bed and sat. "He's good. We're still seeing each other a lot. Would you ever have believed that we both found our guys at the same time?"

"What does he think about Sara and Richard?"

"That's another story. He thinks that Sara should end it with Richard."

"Why?"

Brenda took another candy. "They were good at first, but Sara told Mark that Richard makes her feel uneasy sometimes."

Jess tried to sit up a little more. "What do you mean?"

"His erratic behavior. Sometimes he's in a great mood and sometimes he's down in the dumps. Always complaining about his son. You know Mark is very protective of his mother. He remembers how much she hurt because of his father's abuse and he doesn't want her to go through that again. Not that Richard is abusive, but Mark doesn't want Sara to get involved with Richard's problems—real or imaginary."

"Maybe she should stop seeing him."

"The problem is she really likes him and keeps giving him one more chance."

Jess said, "I hope they work things out. They're both such nice people."

The nurse came into the room, handed Jess her crutches and said, "Let's go, Jessica. Your friend can come along."

The three of them went into the hall and Brenda held Jess's arm. Jess had trouble getting used to using crutches and as she was huffing and puffing, she said, "Hey Brenda, let's train for a three-legged race.

CHAPTER 38

Sam, relieved to see a cop at Frank's door, told Frank's daughters to go in first. He and his boss saw how anxious they were to see him but asked that they keep it short. They understood that Sam wanted to speak to Frank as soon as possible.

When Sam and Jim entered the room, Frank's head and face were heavily bandaged. He seemed to be breathing easily.

Sam asked, "How are you doin', sport?"

Frank opened his eyes and held his hand up—making a circle with his thumb and second finger, signaling OK.

"Are you in a lot of pain?"

Frank shrugged his shoulders.

"Frank, did you recognize the shooter?"

Frank shook his head no.

"Were you holding your briefcase, when you were shot?"

Frank nodded.

"Frank, you told me you found out something of interest about someone you interviewed that day. Can you give me a name?"

Frank tried to form the word and speak, but it was too garbled.

Sam said, "Do you think you can write something?"

Frank nodded.

When Sam handed him a pen and pad, Frank wrote in an almost illegible hand, "RB?"

Sam said, "Would that be Richard?"

Frank gave him the thumbs up sign.

"Richard Benson?"

Frank nodded.

"I can hardly believe it. Are you sure it's the Richard Benson that lives next to Jess?"

Frank shrugged his shoulders.

"Did you find something out after calling his home state?"

Frank nodded.

"If I call his last place of employment, would I be on the right track?"

Another thumbs-up.

"Okay, I'll make the calls."

Jess would know where he's from, but I doubt that she'd be able to tell me where he worked. I'll just have to talk to him.

Sam walked close to his bed, shook Frank's hand and patted his shoulder, "You gave us a hell of a scare, buddy. Feel better soon. We need you."

Sam and Jim left the hospital and Sam said, "I'm going see Richard Benson. I'll try to give him some bullshit reason for my asking him the same questions Frank did. No point in showing our hand."

Jim agreed, "Just call me when you're through, Sam."

Sam almost hit a pedestrian on the way to see Benson. I'd better slow down. Don't need two cops landing in the hospital.

***

At Benson's door, Sam said, "Hi Richard. Can I come in a minute?"

"Sure."

Sam saw a vacuum cleaner in the middle of the living room. Either he's expecting company or he's a clean freak.

"How've you been?"

"I'm good. How are you? How's Jess?"

"Not bad and Jess's coming along. I know that you spoke to my partner about Jess's shooting.

"Yes, I did. Is there a problem?"

"We're just trying to complete our records. I don't know if you've heard, someone shot my partner, Frank."

"That's too bad. How is he?"

"I don't know. It doesn't look too good. He's in a coma, and I'm taking over for him. His paperwork for the condo residents is missing, so I'm revisiting the people he saw here. Could you just answer a couple of questions so we can wind things up?"

They were sitting across from each other and Sam observed Benson tapping his hands on his knees. There were beads of sweat on his face.

Sam asked, "Where'd you live before you came down to the sunbelt?"

"Providence, Rhode Island."

"Ah, the New England weather. Gets kind of chilly there, huh?"

"That's why I'm here."

"You're a lawyer. We can use some good ones in Florida."

"I don't practice down here."

"What's the name of the firm you worked for?"

"I gave your partner all that information."

"I know. But Frank's notes were stolen, and he can't tell me what I need to know.

So you worked at…?"

"John Ingram & Associates."

"Are they in Providence too?"

Richard's right heel was shaking up and down, "Yes."

Sam then asked him a few other things and made more small talk.

"Okay, that's about it for now. Take care, Richard."

"You, too."

After Sam got back to his office and settled behind his desk, he called John Ingram & Associates in Providence. After being transferred to three people, he finally reached Mr. Ingram, Richard's immediate boss.

Sam introduced himself and told him about Frank's injury explaining why Ingram was being contacted again. He asked, "What did you think of Richard Benson?"

"A fine lawyer. I held him in high regard until his wife died."

"What do you mean?"

"I guess you know about his son's disability."

"Yes."

"After Richard's wife died, his personality changed completely. Rude to clients. Went on and on about his misfortunes—his wife's death and son's autism."

Sam said, "Wasn't that understandable?"

"Yes, and we were sympathetic at first. But it got worse. I finally had to speak to him. I asked him to seek professional help."

"Did he take your advice?"

"No. He lost it completely and went into a rage. He started tearing up the place—throwing paper and files around."

"What did you do?"

"I had someone take him home and stay with him until he calmed down."

"Did he see a doctor then?"

"Yes, he did, but he didn't keep most of his appointments, and I could see the same pattern starting again. I convinced him to retire and try a change of scenery."

"Have you heard from him since?"

"No, I haven't."

"Thank you for your help, Mr. Ingram."

When Sam hung up, he thought, "Frank's right. This is interesting. But I need something more."

CHAPTER 39

Sam saw Jess thumping along the hall on her crutches when he came off the hospital elevator. "I think you're ready for the Olympics."

"Almost. Guess what? I can go home today. I just called my parents and they're on their way."

She reached her bed, sat on the edge and gave Sam her crutches. He put the crutches aside, took her in his arms and kissed her all over.

"Hey, hey! There are people here."

"I don't care."

"Well, I do. C'mon Sam." She giggled.

Her parents walked in and her dad was carrying a suitcase. He said with a broad grin, "None of that in public children."

"Sorry. Hi Daddy."

Sam was already looking around and gathering Jess's things. "Are you ready to leave?"

"Almost, I have to sign out downstairs and then, I'm yours."

Maggie said, "I looked through your closet and picked out a dress I think will be comfortable for you."

"Okay. Say fellas, can you wait outside? Maggie and I are going to dress me."

Mr. Gladstone and Sam walked to the waiting room. Sam said, "How about our girl, doesn't she look great?"

"Yes, I thank God every day."

"After I help settle her in, I'm going to the market and buy us the makings of a feast. How does that sound, Mr. Gladstone?"

Sam liked the twinkle in his eye. "It's good you're such a great cook, because Jessica certainly isn't."

"Mr. Gladstone sounds so formal. What do you think I should call you?"

"Whatever you want. Tom—or I wouldn't mind Dad. I always wanted a son after Jessica was born."

"At the risk of sounding mushy, I'll call you Dad."

Jessica wheeled out of her room, and after she was formally discharged, they piled into the car. They arranged Jess in the back seat so she'd be comfortable, and the other three squeezed into the front. Jess's father teased, "It's a good thing Maggie's a little bit of a thing. We'd have trouble fitting if she were fat."

After settling Jess in the condo, Sam took off for the market. He bought a week's worth of the staples they would need and then thought about their special dinner. Jess probably wouldn't want anything too heavy, so I think we'll have a salad, salmon, stir-fried veggies, baked potato with sour cream and bacon bits, chocolate mousse for dessert and of course, wine.

Satisfied with his decisions, he checked out and thought about Richard Benson. I'm glad that Jess has her parents with her. Until I get the bastard that shot her, I'm not comfortable with her being alone. Richard is a suspect all right, but I have to dig deeper to be completely convinced.

***

Jess's eyes brightened when she saw Sam unloading all the bags. "Yay. No more hospital food. What did you get?"

"You'll see."

Sam started to prepare the meal. "Dad, could you help Jess to the bedroom and make her lie down and have a rest. I need the kitchen."

Mr. G. saluted Sam. "Yes sir."

As soon as he started handling food, Sam started to unwind. After chilling the wine, he washed the potatoes and put them in the oven. He prepared the mousse and put it in the refrigerator. Rinsed and dried the crisp greens and made the salad. The fish was readied, adding herbs and butter—setting it aside until it was time for it to be broiled. Because he liked to do things in an organized way, his meal was done in record time. When he started to set the table, Maggie stopped him, "Oh no you don't, go talk to Jess. I'll do this."

"You twisted my arm."

Jess lit up when she saw him, "I was lonely and getting bored."

Sam gave her a long and luxurious kiss. She started to moan, then asked, "What do you think our sleeping arrangements should be?"

"First of all, I need to get Kugel. Will your folks mind him being here?"

"No problem with the dog. It's the other thing."

"I thought about it and what I would like is for us to share this bedroom and your folks share the other one. I hope that they won't have a problem with that."

"I agree but my dad may not like it. He'll just have to deal."

Sam chuckled, "We'll need to be quiet. No more of your moaning and groaning."

"Yuh, and none of your loud 'Baby, baby, baby.'"

Sam grabbed her and kissed her again, "We'll both just have to suffer. And now, I have to get back to my dinner."

As usual, Sam's successful meal inspired compliments and the wine gave them a little buzz. Sam regretted that he had to ruin their optimistic and happy mood. "Listen up, people, I hate to spring this on you, but I need to talk to you about something serious."

Jess's concern showed on her face. "What's wrong?"

"It's about a new suspect in all the shootings."

"Who is it?"

"You're not going to like this. I don't want to say right now. But I can tell you he lives in this building."

"I can't imagine who."

"He's just a suspect now. Nothing sure. But what I want you to do is not have anyone over here for a while. I mean anyone. Just say you're not up to a visit and that you're tired or whatever sounds genuine."

"You mean, like being a prisoner in your own home?"

"Jess, you need to take this seriously. Yes, I would rather that neither you nor your folks leave the condo. When I'm with you, we'll go out and do whatever you want. Understand?"

Jess's father popped up, "Yes, Sam. We understand and I for one agree that it's the wise thing to do."

"Good. Now, dessert anyone?"

CHAPTER 40

Richard registered at the Hotel Colby desk. He used his correct name because there was nothing to hide. I know it's foolish, but I can't keep from feeling I'm being unfaithful to Emily. That thinking will finally change.

Excited about their rendezvous, he agreed with Sara. It was much more romantic this way. The hotel had done everything he asked them to. The room located at the end of the hall with no one in the adjoining one. They'll feel like they were the only people in the world, even for only one night. There were flowers and a beautiful basket of cheese, crackers, strawberries and champagne. The bed turned down. Mints on the pillows.

He heard a key in the door. Unprepared for a sudden shock, he saw a black man with a gun in his hand. "Your lover won't be here this evening. Don't move or I'll have to shoot and you won't know why."

Richard froze. "I won't move. Who are you and why are you doing this?"

The stranger's voice was a soft gurgle. "Who I am isn't important. But I'm doing this because now, you won't have to go see your son, anymore. You're ashamed of him so you hide him. Now he lives with a bunch of strangers. Too bad he's not normal, so you can pay attention to him. I know what kind of father you are. You wish your son could have grown up to be just like you. Then you could show him off. Well, I think he'd be better off without a father. Now, turn around."

"That's not true. I love my son."

"Goodbye Richard."

Shot in the back, the victim fell without another word.

***

After thinking for a moment, The Avenger is reliving the reason Richard Benson and all the other victims had to be punished. The story started many years ago.

They were a family of three and lived in a beautiful big house with two upscale cars in the garage. On the surface, they were a happy family. But when the father's business began to be in trouble and he started to drink, it became different.

After the birth of his son, he started to resent the attention his wife paid to the baby. When that kept up through the following years, he would find things to blame the little boy for. At first, he released his anger by spankings. Later, serious beatings. The boy's mother always tried to curtail the beatings and would threaten to leave him. Then the father behaved for a while.

As his business started to fail, the father became more anxious. One evening, he returned from work and seemed to be in a cheerful mood. After he gave his son candy, the boy allowed himself to be happy.

The father went back to work. The child soon became violently ill. The mother bundled him up and drove him to the hospital. The boy survived.

After questioning the father broke down and confessed that he poisoned the candy. He was desperate and thought only of the insurance money he would receive upon the boy's death.

Even though the father showed great remorse, he was convicted and sentenced to life imprisonment.

After this ultimate betrayal of a child by his parent, The Avenger's torment intensified through the years. The Voice then surfaced. Trusted parents and mentors who abuse innocent children should be punished.

The head of The Avenger tilts sideways. Yes, I know. Now we have to do something about Frank—then we'll be safe.

The Avenger makes a quick and quiet exit. Slips out the door, takes the elevator to the basement, steps out into the alley and runs away.

CHAPTER 41

It was fortunate Jess had a queen-sized bed allowing more room for her, Sam, and Jess's cast. They managed to get some sleep. Jess loved having him with her all night, and when she woke up, she saw Sam bending to kiss her slightly prominent bump. "Hey how about me. Am I going to have competition here?"

"Just more of you to love."

A wave of nausea attacked her. "Sam, please get me something. I need to throw up."

He ran to get the wastebasket from the bathroom.

When she stopped, she said, "I guess I'd better leave this by the bed for the next couple of months. Sorry, honey, I guess the romance is gone."

"Never." He wrinkled his nose, "I love watching you vomit."

He gave her a peck on the cheek. "I've got a lot to do today. I need to get going."

"Anything you can tell me about?"

"Not yet. I will soon enough."

"Be careful Sam."

He showered and dressed. Careful not to wake the parents, he tiptoed out of the condo. Then he went upstairs and rang Mark's bell.

"Hi, Sam. What are you doing here?"

"We brought Jess home yesterday, so I thought I'd come up to talk a little."

"I have to get to work, but I have a few minutes. C'mon in."

They both took a seat on the couch. Sam said, "The shootings have me baffled."

"Can I help with anything?"

"What do you know about Richard Benson?"

"Not a lot. My mother has been seeing him socially, and she talks to me about him sometimes."

"What does she say?" Sam didn't hear a trace of a stammer. It's strange. Sometimes it's quite pronounced. Why not now?

Mark said, "Well, they went out a lot and at first she had a great time, but lately, she says he makes her nervous. He feels sorry for himself and doesn't hide it. Keeps repeating if his son were normal, he'd have a different life. He seems to be very moody lately."

"Moody?"

"Yuh. He's up and then he's down. She thought of breaking up with him, but decided to give him another chance. They made a date to spend the night at the Colby Hotel. I don't approve, but she's a big girl."

Sam decided to confide in Mark and said, "I spoke to his former boss, and he told me he made Richard retire."

"Why?"

"He started to get out of hand and wouldn't accept help."

"What do you mean, "out of hand.""

"First of all, he was rude to the clients and they left the firm. Then he trashed the place. His boss liked him a lot until then. It developed after the wife died. Very suddenly."

"It happens sometimes. I know that for a fact."

"You do? How do you know?"

"I can't talk now. I'm late. Come by tonight. It's important, I need to talk to you.

CHAPTER 42

Sam had to work late and was not sure when he'd be home, so Jess and her parents had an early dinner. She didn't feel like watching TV, so she hobbled to the elevator and went down to see Sara. She walked right in her opened door. "How come your door was open?"

Sara, just coming out of her bedroom, looked disheveled and preoccupied. She said. "I had to throw up in a hurry."

"What's wrong?"

"Nothing. I think I'm coming down with something, and I need to go to bed."

"Oh, I hoped you'd be in the mood for company. Sam's working late. But if you're not feeling well, I'll leave in a few minutes, after I catch my breath. I'm still not used to these crutches."

"Sure, take a seat."

"Say, Sara, what's on your face. It's all streaky."

"I'm removing my makeup and I guess it's half

on and half off."

"But it's very dark. You don't wear makeup that dark."

"What's the difference. Are you rested now?"

"Sara, what's wrong?"

"I just feel lousy."

Jess looked at Sara suspiciously, "Funny, I've never seen you wear pants before. Are they new?"

"Why all these questions?"

"Oh, never mind. I think I'll go now."

"Not so fast, Jessica. Sit back down."

"But you're sick!"

"I'm better now. Do you have any more questions?"

"As a matter of fact, I do. Where have you been?"

"I've been to see Richard."

"Oh, how is he?"

"Not so good."

"What do you mean?"

"I mean, he's dead."

"That's not funny Sara. What are you talking about?"

"I just told you."

"Do you have a fever? I've never seen you like this. Maybe you should go to bed."

Sara said with a disturbing grin. "It's a different side of me Jess. You're a smart girl. I think you can figure it out."

Stunned by a wave of fear, Jess got up to go again, and Sara pushed her down. "Yes, Richard was another uncaring father that had to be eliminated."

"Did you…? Are you…?"

"I did and I am. Let me tell you why. My husband was mean to Mark and tried to kill him when he was just 9 years old. A crazy drunk who didn't give a shit about his son and beat him repeatedly; finally tried to poison him and collect the insurance money afterwards. Unfortunately, I didn't have the guts to murder him before he went to prison."

"Sara, how awful! I had no idea. But what does that have to do with Richard?"

"Let me finish. After that happened, I went nuts. I kept thinking that Mark could have died. They took me away and I was hospitalized for six months. Mark went to my sister's. They said I was bipolar. I underwent psychotherapy and they gave me pills. When they discharged me, they said I'd be okay as long as I kept taking the medication."

"That's nothing to be ashamed of. It's good you got treatment."

"I'm not through, Jessica. Be quiet. I got a secretarial job at a nearby hospital. Then one day someone brought a kid to the hospital. His father beat him to a pulp. I couldn't bear to look at the father, and that's when The Voice told me what to do."

"Sara, did you hurt him?"

Jess found it hard to believe how Sara's persona completely changed. She doesn't sound like the Sara I knew and loved.

Sara opened the side table drawer, took out a gun and pointed it at Jess. "What's the matter with you? Of course! I killed the father, and to tell you the truth, I felt good about it."

When Jess saw the gun, her heart beat so loud she could hear it. Forcing herself to appear calm, she knew she had to keep Sara talking. I need more time. She said, "But you took a life."

"He had to be punished, you can see that can't you?"

Jess felt a lump in her throat. It can't end for me now. Just when I found my soul mate. And the baby. God wouldn't do this to me. He saved the baby before. Our little baby deserves a chance. Jess subconsciously felt her stomach.

Sara interrupted her thoughts. "What are you doing?"

"Sara why would you want to hurt my innocent little baby? Isn't that what you're all about. The baby shouldn't be punished."

"I know it shouldn't. But I have no choice. It's part of you. You're both an accident. What do they call it? Yeah! Collateral damage."

Jess looked at her crutches resting at the side of the couch. Maybe if I could get hold of one, grab it and poke Sara, she'd drop the gun. Too many maybe's. I just have to keep her talking. Jess asked, "What about Richard?"

"I'm getting to that. Shut-up and listen."

Jess pretended to listen while she tried to figure a

way out. Maybe if I pretend I'm miscarrying, Sara might come over to help me. Then I'd grab the gun. Again, too many maybe's. But this whole crazy situation is a bunch of maybe's and if-I-coulds. I'll have to pick one soon and hope it'll work.

Sara waved the gun around while she spoke. "When I started working at Memorial Hospital I saw the little boy, Jerry Dobson, and you know what his father did to him. The Voice said Mr. Dobson had to go. Then Mr. Watkins, who made his son play a football game, causing his brain injury. By the way, when I ran away, I tripped over the damn tree trunk lying in his yard. That's how I sprained my ankle. The third victim, Donald Trent, the so-called Boy Scout leader who molested the kids their parents entrusted to him—an unspeakable crime. He wasn't punished enough for that, just a slap on the wrist. The next, the so-called Father Simpson, a priest, who abused boys and got away with it. It's too bad he could just be punished once."

Jess tried to think. What would Sam do? Probably would have charmed Sara into dropping the gun. He had that wonderful way about him. Everyone loved him. I love him. Just when we have our lives all planned and are so happy. What will he do without me and the baby we made. It's not fair.

Jess had her eyes glued to the gun. "And Frank, what about Frank? He's such a great father and wonderful guy. What did you want to punish him for?"

"Too close to finding me out. He checked all the backgrounds of the people at Memorial where I work. I knew he would have called the Chicago police and the newspapers there and found out about my husband and my mental history."

"You don't know that."

"I do. I found all the notes in his briefcase. They told him the whole story, and I had to get him before he had a chance to figure it out."

"And Richard, he didn't abuse his son."

"No, but he wished he had a normal son. Ashamed of him and sent him off to live with strangers. That's unforgivable."

"So you decided to be judge and jury."

"No, I had to carry out The Voice's wishes. Jess, I hate to do this. I really got to like you a lot."

"Sara, you've been like a mother to me. You need help. Please let me help you."

"It's too late Jess. I'm afraid you won't be able to help anyone. I'm sorry, but I can't let you go."

Sara pointed her gun at Jess again. "Close your eyes and think of something pleasant. It'll be quick."

Jess closed her eyes and prayed. Please, dear God, let me go to heaven and be with my baby. Tears started and she lost the strength to try any of her maybe's.

CHAPTER 43

S am thought about Mark's comment the whole day. What's he going to tell me? Is he the perp? I can't believe it. But who knows? He has his moments of nervous stuttering and keeps pumping me about the open cases. Or will he tell me something more revealing about Richard? Now at Mark's door, he didn't know what to think. Mark said, "Come in, Sam. Please sit down. This may take a while."

They both sat. Mark across from him with his hands laced together and bending forward a little—ready to reveal something important. Sam said, "Okay. Is this about Richard?"

"Not really. This is a story of my childhood. I remember most of it and my mother filled the rest in. I know we told Jess a load of crap about my father. We needed a clean start down here."

Sam said, "You don't have to worry about shading the truth. Everybody does it. But what does it have to do with my investigation?"

Mark held both his hands out in a 'stop' position. "Just be patient. I'll get to it."

"Okay, Okay. Do it your way."

"Our family was fairly happy. My father never loved me like my mother did, but he went through the motions until his business failed and he began to drink."

Where is this leading? Why isn't Mark stuttering?

Mark continued, "He resented the attention my mom paid to me, blamed me for everything and constantly beat me up. Mom couldn't get him to stop."

What a lousy childhood. No wonder he stutters. Why isn't he stuttering now?

"My father needed money and was so desperate, he gave me some candy laced with poison. A loving father, huh? He thought he'd collect money from the insurance he had taken out on me years before. My mother found me unconscious, drove me to the hospital and they saved my life."

Jeeze! Maybe it's him and not Richard.

"My father was sentenced to life imprisonment."

Sam became so nervous, he got up and started pacing. What the hell's goin' on?

Mark continued. "Soon afterwards Mom's personality changed; very moody and acting weird. She went to a psychiatrist. My aunt told me she had a nervous breakdown, and I lived with her for the six months my mother spent in the hospital."

Wait a minute! Sara? She seems so normal.

"After being released, she improved a lot. But every now and then she'd stop talking in the middle of a sentence."

Still no stutter. Is it because he's unloading all of this shit?

"She went to work as a secretary for a doctor at a Chicago hospital. She told me about a young patient beaten by his father and would go on and on about how the kid's father got away with such a light punishment. The father was killed shortly after the boy left the hospital. When she told me about the boy's father's death, she said he deserved it. My mother and other hospital employees were questioned. They were cleared of any involvement. Then we moved to Florida."

Mark went on. "My mother stopped taking her medication because she said it made her feel funny. Lately, she's been having trouble sleeping and is acting strange. Every now and then, I noticed a hesitation in the middle of her sentences. I thought nothing of it at first, and when I asked her about it, she said it was my imagination. But it continued and got worse. I think she's been hearing voices."

"Jess got close to Sara and never mentioned anything like that to me."

"I know. Most people wouldn't have noticed, but I knew her best. When she felt right, those behaviors didn't surface."

Sam's memory jolted back to his investigation of

the Watson murder and when he visited the scene and walked through their backyard with a fallen tree in it. The following day was when he tended Sara's sprained ankle.

Sam's gut churned. Oh, my God! Sara didn't trip over a parking barrier. It was the tree lying in the Watsons' yard.

Then Mark said, "After Jess got shot, I became sick with worry. I knew I had to do something. I love my mother very much. She's a very good person and a wonderful mother to me, but she's sick and we need to stop her. She needs help. Sam, I think she's your serial killer and she's out of control. That's when I decided to talk to you."

Sam pulled out his cell and punched Jess's number. "Hello Dad, let me speak to Jess."

CHAPTER 44

Sam hung up. "C'mon Mark. She's at your mother's."

They took the stairs, sliding down most of them, to get to the condo. Sam saw Jess sitting on the couch and Sara pointing a gun at her. His stomach dropped and his head pounded. He had to do something to divert her attention, so he yelled, "Sara, hold it! I have something very important to tell you."

Sara said, "What are you talking about?"

"You don't want to do this. You love Jessica. Remember? You're sick and not thinking straight."

"I know what I'm doing."

Sara didn't let go of the gun and continued to point it at Jess. Sam kept talking and saying anything that came into his mind. "You love Jess. Sara, remember the nice times you had with her. What fun you had going shopping. And when she asked your advice about us, you were so wise. You don't want to harm the baby, do you? Sara, please give me the gun."

"Stay back. This has to be done."

"Sara why? What good would it do?"

Mark said. "Mom, you know you're sick. We'll get the best people to help you. Please end this now."

"Stay out of this, Mark. Go away!"

While the three of them talked, Sara relaxed her grip on the gun. Jess saw she had a chance to get it. Slowly, she reached over for her crutch leaning on the side of the couch.

Sam noticed what was going on and said, "Sara, Mark's right. You don't want to hurt anyone else. Jess's going to have a baby. You don't want to kill our baby, do you?"

"I can't help it and…"

Jess grabbed her crutch and swung it over to try to make Sara drop the gun. Sara lost her balance and Sam ran over and plowed into her. She rolled away from him and dropped it. Sam reached for it, but Sara grabbed it first. Mark and Jess tried to help subdue Sara, but Jess couldn't manage with one leg and fell. While Sam and Mark were getting her up, Sara broke away and rushed out the door.

Sam asked, "Are you okay Jess?"

"Yes, Go!"

Sara headed toward the stairway and started running to the top floor with Sam and Mark close behind her.

She struggled with the door to the roof but finally opened it, closed it behind her, hid behind one of the air conditioning units and tried to catch her breath. She still had her gun and had it pointed toward the door.

Sam pushed the door open and Mark ran ahead of him. He called, "Mom, where are you?"

Sara said, "Over here."

As he stepped out of Sam's way, Sara took aim and fired at Sam. Hit him in the left shoulder. Mark saw where his mother was hiding and begged, "Mom, please give me the gun."

"No Mark. Now, get out of my way."

"You'll have to shoot me or give me the gun."

While Mark held Sara's attention, Sam was able to crouch down and crawl, using one hand, along to the other side of the roof. He got behind Sara. When he grabbed her, she dropped the gun. He tried to hold her and reached for it, but she pulled away and ran to the edge of the roof.

Mark screamed and rushed toward her. "Mom. Don't!"

She signaled for him to stop and tilted her head to the side. The Voice was back.

She jumped.

EPILOGUE

Five Years Later

"Hurry up, you guys. We don't want to miss Uncle Frank's wedding." Jessica was struggling with her hair trying to tame it enough to get it under her new saucy hat.

"Mommy, mommy, Joey keeps pulling my bow." Ruthie, her five-year-old daughter, came crying into her parent's bedroom, followed by her twin. As soon as Jess saw them, she forgot about her hair and sat them down on her bed. After she scolded Joey, she gave them both a hug and sent them downstairs.

She still felt blessed by the life she had now. Full of love and laughter. Just as she had imagined it. When they found out about the twins, she and Sam were ecstatic. After a rocky pregnancy and a lot of bedrest, their two perfect beautiful children were born. And now every day that goes by reminds them how lucky they are.

Sam walked into the bedroom. "Jess, can you help me with this tie."

"I suppose so." She fixed his bow tie, gave him a kiss and a pat. "Now go down and wait with the kids. I need to do something with my hair."

Jess contemplated their last few years. Their twins, Ruth, named after her mother and Joe after Sam's father. All the joy they brought them. Then, Mark's getting over his mother's death. His marriage to Brenda, and the birth of their child. And today, Frank was marrying the nurse he met when he was in the hospital. Life was going on.

When she heard the start of another family disagreement downstairs, she plopped her hat on and ran down. She did a double take when she saw her family waiting—her little girl with curly hair and bright blue eyes, her son, the spitting image of his father and, Sam, the love of her life. "Sam, you look soo sexy in that tux."

"What's sexy, mamma?" Ruthie asked.

"Never mind. Let's go."

Jess asked, "Do you have your toast notes?"

"Nah, I'll wing it."

They got to the church and Sam went out back to be with Frank. Jess and the children joined Brenda and Mark, who held seats for them. The music started and Mark and Brenda were fidgeting. Jess reassured them. "Don't worry. It'll be fine."

The small procession started and when everyone stood up for the bride, a little 3-year-old appeared

leading the bride's way with a path of rose petals—
walking as she was told. A slow cadence. When she
reached the point where her parents were cheering
her on, she turned toward them, and little Sara Janus smiled and waved before continuing.

About the Author

B F Jochnowitz, born and educated in Boston, Massachusetts, has always had a passion for writing. Alongside her husband, she co-owned and operated a publishing firm in Marblehead, Massachusetts, specializing in the editing and typesetting of college textbooks. After relocating to Florida, she penned her first book, "A POLISH BOY: The Youngest Partisan," as a tribute to her husband's life. She is currently working on a series of mystery novels set to be published in the near future.

www.ingramcontent.com/pod-product-compliance
Lightning Source LLC
Chambersburg PA
CBHW060313260626
47160CB00007B/2588